Room Four

By

A.J. Knauss

Copyright © 2012 A.J. Knauss
All rights reserved.
ISBN: 1477572430
ISBN 13: 9781477572436

Dedicated to Esther Davis, who taught me what the textbooks didn't.

A portion of the sale of this book will be donated to the Sojourner Truth House in Esther's memory.

Chapter 1

I died in the second half of the Bears versus Vikings game. The one when the Bears beat Minnesota. Of course I didn't learn the score until much later. Had to look it up. But I'll get to that. It was supposed to be a monumental game. The Packers' quarterback had defected to the Vikings and that meant Wisconsin fans were rooting for the Chicago Bears, which was unheard of. So my sudden change in color to blue and my slumping back on the couch probably went unnoticed for a few minutes. That's my best guess anyway. A little warning would have been nice. But no. A lethal arrhythmia is apparently a silent event. My wife and I, we were over at a friend's place in the city and I think that's when it happened. What happened after that, well, it's a long story. I'll tell you what I remember.

"Hey, student-what's-your-name."
"Me?"
"Yes, you. You know how to do CPR?"
"Um, yes."
"Good. Take over here. I'm getting tired."
"But I've never done it on a real person."
"That's OK. This guy's dead. You can't make him more dead."

I watched the young man step onto a stool, position his hands and push on the man's chest. There was a group of people and a flurry of activity, clustered under the glare of two circular fluorescent lights. A young woman had a tourniquet on the man's arm and she filled tube after tube of blood, seemingly oblivious to the guy leaning over her pushing on the man's sternum.

"Are we doing hypothermia protocol?" asked the first man. I rubbed my eyes. He was wearing one of those headbands that had reindeer antlers sticking out the top. The younger man, the one doing CPR, had an elf hat on with oversized ears on each side and they bounced up and down as his head bobbed. Was it Christmas, I thought, no, it was January. The football game. I was watching football.

"Yep. Vfib arrest. He meets the criteria. But wait until we see if there is any return of circulation before we ice him down."

"Another round of epi then?"

"Give it."

"Last atropine."

"He's maxed on atropine already? OK, give it."

I leaned on the wall on the side of the room and wondered how I had gotten here. There were three young men in short white coats standing next to me. One jotted down notes in a spiral notebook. One was playing something on his phone. The third seemed to be actually paying attention to the proceedings.

"See those two? They have a thing."

There was an old man leaning on the wall on the other side of me. He wore a rumpled flannel shirt and olive-green corduroy trousers hiked over his paunch with a battered old belt. He had one of those vests with all the pockets on it like the things photographers wore.

"Who are you?" I asked.

"Name's Gerald, Gerald Verne. You can call me Jerry. Anyway. See those two. The short nurse and the guy, the doctor? They have a thing."

"OK. A thing. That's great. Look, I'm not sure how I got in here but I don't think I'm supposed to be here. I'm not feeling so well. I think this must be a private matter. Is there a door on the other side of the curtain?"

The old man laughed loudly. No one surrounding the gurney seemed to notice. "That's pretty good. I wasn't supposed to be here today either, although I spent enough time in this damn place already. You don't have to make an appointment for this, you know," he chuckled and then gave me a strange look as if I had missed his joke. "Look at them. The holidays are over, you know, I'm surprised they still let them wear that to work. Not too professional in my opinion." He gestured at the reindeer and the elf. He opened up a drawer on the cart next to the gurney. It was filled with labeled vials. Jerry took out one and rolled it across the top of the cart toward the doctor he had already pointed out. He didn't notice it.

"Narcan, you dumb ass," he said.

There still was no reply.

I watched Jerry pick up a box of bandages and poke the other man in the side of the neck.

"What the?" He turned around and Jerry rolled the vial past him again.

"Let's give him two milligrams of narcan," the doctor said, as he adjusted his collar and looked over his shoulder.

"Isn't that what they use on drug overdoses?" I asked.

"No offense," Jerry said. "You seem nice enough. But they try narcan on everybody. It's worth a try. And if genius here would pay less attention to the nurses maybe he would remember."

"No offense taken. Hey, it was nice talking with you but I don't think I want to watch anymore of this." I was feeling dizzy and frankly a little disoriented. This old guy next to me didn't look like a doctor.

"Stop CPR. Good. Excellent. He has a strong femoral pulse. Olson!" barked the doctor.

"Huh?" said one of the short coat trio.

"How many interns do we need standing around at a code? Olson, get me a blood pressure reading and we'll go ahead with the hypothermia protocol."

"Well, look who came back," Jerry said, with a big pat on my back. "You might be leaving here after all."

The crowded room thinned out as the CPR stopped. And there on the gurney was a man who looked just like me. Exactly like me. I reached out my hand instinctively and grabbed Jerry's arm, my mouth dry and speechless.

"Now you get it. Maybe the narcan worked. Did you shoot up? Is that what it was? I hear heroin is making a comeback."

"What are you talking about? But it's not possible. That's not me. That guy. That guy isn't me."

"It's not possible that you shot up? Do you snort it instead? I thought younger kids did that. Pills and what not. They used to tell me I could have made a fortune if I'd sold my pain meds on the street."

"You think I'm a heroin addict?"

"I'm just trying to help out. Not here to judge."

"That's not me. It's not possible."

I watched as the one of the nurses returned to the room with four large ice packs. She placed two in my armpits, two in the groin. "Should I go ahead with the temperature probe foley?"

"What the, she can't grab my, that thing looks like a garden hose," I was stammering as Jerry held me back.

"Take it easy. I'm sure it comes as a shock. You're young, right, what are you, about fifty?"

"She's packing my testicles in ice! How am I supposed to take this easy? And she, she has tattoos and a bunch of earrings and did you see the guy with the elf ears? Do they just let anybody work here?"

I knew I was grasping at straws but sometimes when one complains it's more effective to give them a litany. It was dawning on me that I might have a lot to complain about. If you're lucky, one item might get resolved and of my list of complaints while being dead was the first one, having my testicle packed in ice was a close second.

A young man in a polo shirt picked up a plastic bag full of clothes. "Is that his too?" he asked, pointing at a cell phone on the metal tray.

"Yep," said the nurse with the garden hose.

"What's that?" he asked, picking up the case.

"Probably one of those cell phone holsters for his belt," she said.

The man rolled his eyes and put everything in the bag. "This guy sure carried a lot of pens."

The old man smiled at me. "Look, you're only half dead. Or maybe all the way dead. I've never seen this hypothermia thing in action before. But it's supposed to help. Cool down your brain while the rest of you heals up. You might be back in the old bod before you know it."

"No, no, no, no. This is not happening."

"Oh, it already happened."

"Who are you, Saint Peter or something?"

The old man sighed. "I told you. I'm Jerry. I died on the way upstairs. I think it's a paperwork glitch. Long story. What's your name anyway?"

"Fries. Alan Fries. It's spelled like 'french fries' but it's pronounced 'freeze' like in 'cheese'."

"You always introduce yourself that way? Alan Fries as in Cheese? That would be handy if you were a cheese salesman. I don't suppose you are? Or were, I should say."

"I think I'm going to pass out," I said.

Jerry laughed again. "I don't know if you can do that when you're dead. Listen, if you want to watch something other than Nurse Rachet putting the garden hose in your schlong, I'm going to head over to the nurse's station and figure out how I got stuck here in the first place."

I followed the old man numbly past the curtain, willing myself to wake up from the dream. The curtain was pulled halfway and as the crowd circulated around the bed I caught glimpses of feet, pale, still and unmoving at the end of the bed. My feet. The same man who had been running the resuscitation was now shouting into the phone. He was balding and wore wire rimmed glasses. "I told you already," he said, emphasizing each word as if he was talking to a two year old. "I admitted him upstairs. I admitted him to Dr. Leak and he was accepted by Dr. Leak. He wasn't in great shape when he left here but he was going to palliative care. He died under Dr. Leak's care, seven floors above my head. I am not going to fill out a death certificate when I don't know how he died."

The phone buzzed in response and I couldn't help but lean in with Jerry to hear the response.

"We can't bring him back down to room 4. We have another patient in room 4. A live patient. And putting him in a bunk bed with a dead guy would be bad for morale."

The buzzing on the phone went up an octave.

"It's not my fault that Dr. Leak isn't fast enough to actually go see his patients before they die. Maybe this will light a fire under him to be a little more conscientious. No. No, it doesn't change things that he died on our gurney. Oh, so he wasn't moved over into the bed-type bed and so therefore he is still in the emergency department? Even though he went into an elevator and went seven stories up to palliative care? This department doesn't extend that far. Call Dr. Leak. He needs to do the death certificate." The phone slammed down. The doctor looked up at the acoustic tiled ceiling. "Why do I work with morons?" he asked. He turned his attention to the CPR student.

"Hey, Santa's Helper."

"Who, me?"

"Yes, you with the ears. Take those off when the family gets here. In fact take them off now. It sends the wrong message."

"What message?" asked the student as he folded the hat and ears into his lab coat pocket.

"The wrong message. We're not supposed to have fun at work. Saving lives. And you don't want this guy's family to forever associate elves with ventricular fibrillation. Who knows what kind of Pavlovian response that could set up. Besides I want you to come with me when I go meet the family. You need practice in delivering that kind of news."

The student was wide-eyed with the beginning of a smile. "Dr. Maglio, you want me to talk to the family about what happened?"

"Hell no. I want you to stand there, be silent, and look concerned. But you can learn something from me about how to deliver bad news."

"But he's alive. It's not exactly bad news."

The older doctor frowned. "You're a cup half full kind of guy, aren't you? That's OK. I'm sure he'll pull through just fine and go home still able to do the Sunday crossword puzzle."

"But he has a pulse. His blood pressure is better."

"Takes more than a pulse to do the crossword puzzle," said the doctor, "but maybe just a pulse to get into medical school these days," he added under his breath.

A woman in a lab coat looked up from her computer. "Maglio, give the kid a break."

"She's the boss," whispered Jerry. "She's the only one who can put up with all their crap."

"Whose crap?" I asked.

"All the staff's crap. You spend enough time here; you'll get to know them."

"If you know all the staff here then who was the guy doing CPR on me?"

"That guy? Him I don't know. Probably an intern or a medical student. From the way Dr. Maglio was talking I would guess he was a student."

"Wait a minute. Aren't interns the lowest people on the totem pole? That's who they had circulating blood to my vital organs?"

"Actually the students are lower than the interns. But don't worry about it. CPR is the easy part. If you spend more time in the ER you'll see the decisions are the hard part. That's why I decided I didn't want CPR. After enough poking and prodding, well, let's just say I knew when I was done. Do not resuscitate." He held up his wrist which was adorned by a medical alert bracelet. "They put it on the bracelet. I told them to tattoo it on my forehead but they wouldn't do it. You had a great nurse working on you, by the way. She's a peach. She's who I would pick if I needed the garden hose. But I've always had a tip top prostate. About the only part of me that didn't crap out."

I was going to tell Jerry that I didn't want to spend any more time here than I already had but that seemed to be beside the point.

"Don't tell me to fill it out," said a voice from behind me. I turned. It was the balding doctor with the wire rimmed glasses again.

"Maglio, would it matter?" It was the woman in the lab coat.

"Yes it would matter. It would matter that Dr. Leak is a lazy piece of crap that wants the ER to do all his work."

"But he never saw him. The guy died on our gurney. You know his medical history. How hard would it be to fill out the stupid form?"

Dr. Maglio folded his arms across his chest and spun around in the chair. "It's the principle. And besides, how do I know how he died? For all I know Leak came and put a pillow over his head and then I would be an accessory to murder."

The director sighed and pushed her glasses down her nose. She had a brown lunch bag in front of her on the desk and a half-eaten saran-wrapped peanut butter sandwich sitting on top of it.

"Oh, for God's sake, get over it. Jerry Verne was older than dirt, we've all taken care of him a hundred times and he had terminal cancer. He had a lot of reasons to die. Pick something plausible like respiratory arrest or even old age if you want to and fill in the blank. Someone is going to fill out the paperwork. I don't care if it is you or Leak but I don't want to see anything about this in my email tomorrow."

Maglio mumbled something and turned back to his computer.

"I mean it, Maglio. I'm not even supposed to be working this shift, you know. McCallister called in sick again with a sore throat. Give me a break. I had an arterial bleed in room 10, and open ankle in 2, and I have to go do a central line on the four hundred pounder with gangrene in room 9. You know, if the nurse takes off your sock and three toes just fall off, you've probably waited too long to come to the ER. But if you call an ambulance because you stubbed your toe drunk, you probably haven't waited long enough. Yesterday was the drunk. Today it's the guy whose toes just fell off. That was something that honestly, even for me; I could have lived without seeing. Anyway, I wish the drunk guy was still here so I could wheel him into the room and give a lecture on abuse of the 911 system."

"I'll keep that in mind," Maglio smiled. "You know, we framed a sock once and gave it to one of the faculty when I was in training. One of the regulars in the ER donated it."

The director scoffed. "You actually stole a sock from a passed out drunk in your ER? That's low."

"What are you implying? I said he donated it. Out of appreciation for the institution that had kept him alive on IV thiamine for so many years. At least I didn't call in sick with a sore throat. If I call in sick it's because I'm dead. And then I won't call. Anyways, we framed the sock in a shadow box to encase the smell and got a plaque that said 'The Toxic Sock Award' and gave it to the professor. I've been back. He still has it in his office."

"That's great. I knew I hired you for your love of humanity. By the way?" She was on her feet now and shrugging out of her white coat in preparation for the procedure and she looked down her glasses at the other doctor. "Do the paperwork."

"Did three toes really fall off?" asked Maglio.

"Yes. Don't remind me. And don't change the subject," replied the director.

"Did McCallister really call in sick with a sore throat again?"

"Yes. And giving me sympathy won't work. You still need to do the paperwork. But I might have to kill McCallister and then he would really have a reason to call in sick. I think he's probably out on an interview. Can't blame the guy. By the way, are you coming to St. Pat's with me?"

"I can't decide. I still think I might go back to the academic center."

The director rolled her eyes. "But you hate teaching. And you hate interns."

"So do a lot of other people in the academic center. That's a good thing. The interns pick up the vibe and they don't stay interns very long."

The director shook her head. "And I thought that model of teaching went out with the dinosaurs."

"It's effective. And they can do the procedures. Or at least deal with the gangrenous toes. And yes, I will do the paperwork. After I catch up on these other charts," he gestured at a stack in front of him. "These people are still alive so someone might want to read it sooner."

"Actually the joint commission is supposed to be here this week. And you know how rational their priorities are. They always pull a chart on a recent death. If they don't see a complete chart on this guy they'll accuse us of leaving his body parked in the hallway or something. If it's not documented on paper it didn't happen, right?"

Dr. Maglio groaned. "Do you know what day they're going to be here?"

"I know not the hour or the day," began the director.

"Stop sounding like the pope."

"Actually I think it was scripture that predates the pope."

"Whatever. If I have to work on the day they're here I will stab my eyeballs out with a fork."

"Maglio, it's not that bad. The worst thing you have to do is keep a lid on your coffee cup and not eat food at the computer. I actually have to meet with them."

"And I have to run laps around the department trying to find the nurse who has the key to the supply cabinet that we lock once a year in honor of the joint commission. That's the worst part. Pretending that locking up all the gauze is going to improve patient safety. Can I stab them with a fork? Would I be covered under the malpractice plan if I did?"

"Maglio, I am the choir," said the director, "and you are preaching to me. How about you just get your paperwork done? And please don't stab anybody."

"Wherever I work next," said Maglio, "I'm going to pick a less sanctimonious medical director."

"Bite me," she said.

Jerry was beaming. He pounded me on the back and I barely felt it. I really had to wake up from this. "A glitch! It really is all due to a paperwork glitch. I'll be damned."

"You shouldn't say that when you're dead."

"Good point Cheesy"

"It's Fries. Alan Fries. Like…"

"Like cheese. Yes, I know. You told me already. Do you mind if I call you Cheesy instead?"

"Actually, I do mind. Today has been bad enough without whoever you are calling me what I used to get called on the playground."

"You're kidding."

"I'm not. The other kids called me Cheesy."

"Well, gee Alan. Maybe it's because you introduce yourself as Fries-like-cheese all the time. Anybody ever point that out to you?"

"No. It's just what rhymes. Besides, I was tired of being called French-fries before that. What's the big deal?"

"Nothing. No big deal. Except it clearly bothers you enough to bring it up immediately in conversation even after you're dead."

"I'm not dead. This is a dream. Or a misunderstanding. Or it's just what happens when they shock your heart and put that breathing machine thing on. It's like anesthesia. People get all kind of weird hallucinations under anesthesia. I've read about it. Anyways, I didn't bring it up. You asked if you could call me Cheesy."

"And you introduced yourself as Cheese. That's how I remember stuff. What is that called, a moniker?"

"No, it's a mnemonic," I replied.

"Mnemonic. Mnemonic. I always forget that word," said Jerry.

"I can't believe this."

"I can't believe you introduce yourself as Fries-as-in-cheese your whole life and wonder why you have a nickname. A lot of other things rhyme with your name you know. Trees for one. Then you could have been called Tree on the playground. You're pretty tall anyways. Me Alan. Big Tree. Not a bad thing. How about I just call you Cheese for short?"

"Just leave me alone. I need to wake up. This is a bad dream. A really weird one. I must have fallen asleep on the couch watching the game."

"I wonder how much time I have?" mused Jerry. He reached behind Dr. Maglio to the nurse that was bringing him the chart from room 4. She had teal green scrubs on with a pair of short shorts pulled over them that said "ho, ho, ho" across the backside. I watched in shock as Jerry pulled the ties loose on her scrub pants. "Hey!" she said to Maglio sharply.

"I think they have a thing too. Those two in your room? You know, the one that doesn't know his ass from a hole in the ground and the nurse that had the garden hose? They definitely have a thing but I think these two have a thing too. A glitch. This is giving me all kinds of ideas. I think I have the run of the place until they sign me off."

He was whispering again. He leaned on the doctor's shoulder who was oblivious to the weight of the old man.

"If we're really dead, you probably don't need to whisper," I said.

Jerry cocked his head and seemed to be sizing me up. He laughed. "Good point. You seem to be catching on quick. So what are we going to do with this interlude? That's the real question. These guys hate paperwork. This might take weeks. And you, who knows how long you have?"

"You're awfully cavalier about this."

"I know. I know. I shouldn't be so hard on you. You weren't expecting to die today. Me, I've spent so much time in this damn place I thought I would have died a year ago. Cancer, kidney failure, you name it. Of course I don't shoot heroin. You really should be careful with the hard stuff," he added, patting me on the shoulder.

"I am not a drug addict!"

"Then why did the narcan work? Last I saw, you had a pulse and were headed to full resuscitation. Sounds like poppies to me."

"I'm sure they give that to everyone."

"That's what they all say."

"Jerry I am not even going to have an argument with you about this. They were doing CPR at the time too, in case you didn't notice. And they used the ice pack thing and whatever else. I'm sure it was more high tech than it looked. Anyway, the narcan was probably a coincidence. I thought I asked you to leave me alone."

Jerry was still wagging his finger at me. "It's a second chance to stop the hard stuff."

"I'm not dignifying that with a response," I replied.

The phones rang nonstop all around us. Monitors beeped, pagers alarmed, overhead announcements came through the PA system. I didn't understand how anyone could work here. It reminded me of the floor of the stock exchange, a place I had visited as a college kid only once. It took only one visit to convince me my temperament was not suited to be a trader. The ER was like the stock exchange but worse. And nobody seemed to be paying any attention to the alarms.

The secretary in the middle of the ER took yet another call.

"St. Augustine's emergency department. Yes. Yes, I remember you. I know you called earlier. I asked them. They haven't found them yet. I have your number. Yes. I will call you if we hear anything. I understand they're unusual. We certainly want to return them if they are found. Yes. We'll try our best."

Maglio looked her way after she put the phone down.

"What was that about?"

"Nipple rings. Thinks they got lost in x-ray."

"Did you see the patient? Is she cute?"

"No. And it's a guy. And I don't know if he's cute."

Chapter 2

Two cops leaned against the counter. They both held Styrofoam cups of coffee. They seemed surprisingly oblivious to the guy behind them shouting obscenities about their mothers. And they certainly were oblivious to us.

"You know how much longer we got to wait before we take this guy to the enchanted kingdom?" the one asked the other. The older cop turned around and looked at their charge. He was hard to miss. Handcuffed to the gurney, purple sequined dress, a full beard and a cowboy hat, he was making crazy a fashion statement.

"Might be hours. Psych beds are backed up when it's this cold out. Three hots and a cot beat the street so they all start acting crazy to get a foot in the door."

"Overtime, then. This is great."

The older man slurped the dregs of the cup. "Sure is."

"You married?" Jerry startled me. I thought one of the cops had noticed me. Cops made me nervous even when I wasn't dead. The last time I thought I was going to get off with just a warning I ended up with a speeding ticket and I had to get out of the car and walk in a straight line. My wife was in the passenger seat at the time. She told me later that I started sweating so much after the cop asked me for my license that it looked like I was on cocaine. I asked her later how she would have known that after I sufficiently calmed down and she told me she saw it in a movie. But it made me wonder. She had a wilder time in college than I did. Sociology major. I think she whitewashed a few details.

I took a deep breath. "Yes."

"Kids?"

"Two. They're pretty much grown up." I wondered how they would take it. Laura would call them. She probably had called them already. They both were in college out of state. My timing was terrible. They had both just been home for a week for winter break. I wondered if they could get discounts on plane tickets for a genuine emergency. If I could put the tickets on my rewards card I would at least get some cash back out of this mess. 1% of emergency plane tickets were better than chump change. As if I could tell them to use my card. My wallet was in a plastic bag somewhere along with my cell phone. That security guard had some nerve cracking jokes about my cell phone holster. It happened to be a very useful item.

"They're good kids," I said. "Are you married?" I asked him.

"Was. Widowed. Millie died about ten years ago. I'm eighty-seven you know."

"I'm sorry to hear that. About your wife, that is. Not about being eighty-seven."

"I was lucky to have her. We had it good. She was something else. The last ten years, getting to eighty-seven, I don't know if I would call that part luck. We got married right after the war. Wouldn't mind meeting up with her if that's still the way it goes after doc signs the paperwork. How old are you?"

"I'm fifty-two."

"Fifty-two," Jerry said thoughtfully. "I remember when I was in my fifties. Millie and I went to Cuba for our twenty-fifth wedding anniversary. Boy, did we put away some drinks. She had the best little swim suit then. She was something."

"But you can't go to Cuba. Americans can't go there."

"No rules against it then. What a great country. Place is probably a mess now. I don't know. Where did you go for your twenty-fifth?"

"Go?" I stammered. It was not a piece of detail I thought I would need to dredge up at that particular moment, especially if

I needed a story to compete with a forbidden island getaway. "We went to that one restaurant downtown, the one that rotates while you eat."

Jerry harrumphed. "Overpriced. Foods never as good as the price but I suppose you're paying for the novelty."

"Well we enjoyed it," I replied. The truth was I couldn't remember what we had done for our twenty-fifth anniversary and it was bothering me. It hadn't been that long ago. Laura wasn't really one to hold forgotten things over my head like some wives I knew. And I was pretty good with remembering dates. Except that time I was out of town on her birthday and I called to say hello and didn't mention it. And her mother was visiting for the week that I was away and Laura told her I had forgotten. And then her mother called me back to let me know what she thought about a man leaving town on business and forgetting his wife's birthday. And by the time she called back, I was out at the meet and greet reception for Graham and Graham. I put my cell phone on speaker before because I had needed my hands free to do my tie while Laura and I talked. It was a new phone and I was never very good at figuring out the features. Touch screens and tiny buttons were designed for people with smaller fingers, maybe toothpicks for fingers. So my phone was still on speaker when my mother-in-law called back. And I dropped it into my artichoke dip appetizer while fumbling around to take it off speaker, to the delight of my colleagues.

But Laura would remember what we did for our twenty-fifth anniversary. I hope it had been something good. What if she asked me when I came to? She might ask to prove to the rest of the family that my faculties were all still intact and I would fail miserably.

"You know your family has the football game on in room 4, don't you?"

"What?!"

I left Jerry standing over the two who may or may not have a thing and ran back toward room 4. The curtain was pulled but I could hear the game before I even stepped inside.

"The Vikings are down. It's about time," it was my friend Kevin.

Laura was a mess. She had probably been crying on the way here. I reached out my hands instinctively. She sniffed, "But they still could get a field goal." She looked toward me, the me that was on the bed, that is. "Honey, the Vikings are down."

Garden-hose nurse with the tattoos came in the room. "I'm sorry Mrs. Fries," she said. "Would you like me to turn this off? Someone must have turned it on from housekeeping when Mr. Fries was over in the CT scanner."

"It's Fries-as-in-cheese, not fries as-in-french-fries," Laura said.

"Sorry, Mrs. Fries."

"That's all right. And you can leave the TV on."

"We thought he would like to hear the game, if he can hear at all in there," said Kevin.

"Of all the pompous pricks. Who is that guy?" Jerry had caught up with me.

"Jerry, it's OK," I said.

"No it's not. Did you hear what he said? He's a pompous prick and he's ogling your wife."

"Can you give it a rest? Kevin is my friend. We were watching the game together. He lives near here."

"Ogling."

"Nobody ogles at a time like this."

"Why not? You've got a few things to learn. It's the perfect time to ogle. We thought he might like to hear the game. What a bunch of nonsense. I feel your pain. What a line. He's doing the sympathy ploy. You shouldn't let him get away with it."

"Drop it, Jerry."

"What if he offers to drive her home?" Jerry asked.

"I said to drop it."

Jerry sighed, frowning. "She is a looker, by the way."

"Thank you," I answered drily.

"Where are the kids?" he asked.

"They're both away at school. College."

"Two kids in college at the same time? No wonder you keeled over. That's got to be some bill."

"Jerry, its fine."

"They studying anything useful?" he asked.

"They haven't declared majors. Neither has. Look, since you know this place so well, why don't we go somewhere else? I think I need a break."

"Great idea. How about the nurse's locker room?"

"For an old geezer, you act like you're twelve," I said.

"What am I supposed to act like? The ghost of Christmas past? Rattle some chains and grant you three wishes? Is that the elephant in the room?"

"No, the elephant in the room is that I'm stuck here talking to a dead guy when I am supposed to be home watching the Vikings get their rear end kicked. And I don't think the ghost of Christmas past grants wishes. I think that was Aladdin. And don't get me started on my other problems," I said.

"That maybe you're dead problem?" Jerry asked.

"That seems to be the main one."

"I think your problem is you mix metaphors. It was Aladdin's lamp, by the way. Aladdin was just the guy who picked it up. Attention to detail. Maybe that's why your kids are English majors. What did you do when the game was on, choke on a chicken wing or something?"

"You tell me. Last thing I know I was watching the Vikings play the Bears. And they aren't English majors. They're undeclared."

"Same thing," Jerry said.

I followed Jerry back into the main ER. Maglio and the director were still arguing but this time it was about something different.

"I don't know who approved the mural. Amazing isn't it? For four years I can't get proper trauma resuscitation support. The only patients we're seeing more of are moribund nursing home patients that Dr. What's-his-mug admits for physical therapy. They dump our contract and now they decide to paint a mural in the entryway," said the director.

"That thing is costing five grand in labor easily," said Maglio.

"Med Prompt. Did you say, call Dr. Waverly?" said a tinny voice emanating from Dr. Maglio's shirt pocket.

"No," Maglio said.

"OK," said the voice cheerfully. "Let's try again. Med Prompt. Who should I call?"

"Your mother," Maglio said.
"I didn't understand. Let's try again. Med Prompt."
"Bite it," said Maglio.
"OK, I'm calling Dr. Lighte."
"No," said Maglio.
"Let's try again. Med Prompt."
"Log out," Maglio roared.

The director heard him from across the room where she had gone to watch the mural painting. "You can't log out of Med Prompt in the middle of a shift."

"Then how else do I make the damn thing shut up?" asked Maglio.

"It probably bumped a pen in your pocket and activated. Just give it a minute," she said.

"Med Prompt. Med Prompt" came the tinny little voice again.

"Why don't you wear the ear piece? It doesn't broadcast for the whole ER to hear if you wear the earpiece," said the director.

"Like I want that directly in my ear? The voice activated system that can't identify anything intelligible? If anything might push me over the edge in this place, that might be the very thing," replied Maglio as he pulled an oval shaped receiver out of his pocket and discreetly slipped off the battery pack. He dropped both back into his pocket and looked back at the computer screen.

Another phone line rang over the beeping monitors, alarms, and four other ringing phone lines which were currently on hold and beeping.

"Dr. Maglio, it's your wife on line seven," said the secretary.

He sighed and looked up at the acoustic ceiling tiles for a long moment before picking up the phone. "Hi, Hon. Yep. I have it. Yep. I'll drop it off this afternoon. I know. Last night. When you were sleeping. Well excuse me; I had to get it done, right? Yes, I was thinking of you. There's a fridge here. Well, it's good enough. When? They'll probably let me know tomorrow or so. I know. OK. I'll see you tonight."

Maglio hung up and was pensive for a moment.
"You know what I want?"

I winced at the voice and instinctively crossed my legs. It was Nurse Garden-hose. "I want a big fat trauma to come in right now. Right now when that skinny painter bitch on her iPod is up on the ladder painting little swirlies and fish and whatever else on the mural. I want a big fat gunshot wound to get dropped off at triage and to come right down our new entryway, stagger into the wall, splash some blood on the mural and knock that skinny bitch off her ladder. And when she climbs back up, she can paint 'Welcome to Holy Tino's' right above the blood splatter. Wouldn't that be perfect?"

"True, you're seriously disturbed but I love you," said Dr. Maglio.

"Med Prompt. Calling Dr. Aiwoo," came a tinny voice from True's scrub shirt pocket.

Maglio groaned. "Not you too. When did the nurses get those infernal things?"

"Last week," said True.

"I didn't understand," said the voice. "Let's try again. Med Prompt."

"I thought it might be helpful at first. Voice activated technology. Order labs and talk to pharmacy and all that. It sounded way better than a zone phone. But it's worse. Worse than, hmm, it's worse than a nurse intern. It's like carrying a demented preschooler around in your pocket all day. The thing can't understand any of the voice prompts. But it's always happy anyway," said True.

"Med Prompt," said the voice again. "Let's try again."

"For the love of God already, I have four kids. I don't have time to play with this thing too. Try again, play with me, what should we do today, you love me, I'm Barney the dinosaur?" True mimicked the awkwardly chipper tones of the receiver. "Has this thing seriously been on the market for five years?"

"They forgot about the concept of ambient noise when they bought the system for the ER," said the director. "It works OK in other parts of the hospital so they assumed it would work here. Supposedly the IT department is working on making them less sound sensitive."

"Less sound sensitive? That's their answer? So then I can yell at it louder when I really have to call someone?" mused Maglio.

"Hey, I didn't buy them," said the director.

"Med Prompt. Calling Dr. Bidem,"

"No!" said the director, speaking toward her shirt pocket.

"OK, let's try again. Med Prompt."

"Log out."

"You can't log out in the middle of a shift," pointed out Maglio.

"Really? What are they going to do? Fire me?" asked the director as she stalked away.

True laughed. "What was all that about with your wife on the phone anyways?"

"Long story."

"Are they the ones that have a thing?" I asked Jerry.

"No, that's the other guy."

"You know it's only a matter of time before Raymond comes in and pees on it," said True.

"On what?"

"On the mural."

"Who's Raymond again?" asked Maglio.

"You know Raymond Ray. He's the guy who keeps getting picked up because some citizen sees him passed out on the sidewalk and calls 911."

"We see a lot of those guys."

True leaned on the counter. "The one with the broken nose that goes in three different directions"

"The guy that always tries to stuff his coat with linens before he leaves?"

"And anything else you leave in the room. That guy."

Maglio smiled. "He's not that bad. For a five foot tall lunatic he's a fighter. I don't know how nobody's killed him off on the street. He's got a mouth. Maybe we could steer him toward the joint commission."

"Easy for you to say. You never had to hose him down with security in the decon shower. We have all this hazmat gear for some terrorist attack right? Costs who knows what to get it installed. And we use it to clean up Raymond," said True.

"Do you want me to get started on investment decisions this hospital administration has made? Because I can," the director chimed in. She had returned from leaving her Med Prompt in the charging station. "Like buying Med Prompts for this zoo. You know they forgot to install floor drains in that decon room right? Two years of arguing and finally the federal regulations that I reminded them of won out and they had to jackhammer up the floor. Because I thought toxic waste runoff probably shouldn't overflow and spill all over the ER floor. Especially not if we are hosing off the drunks in there. In theory. Two years to get that point across. But next time you see Raymond, please steer him that way. In fact, tell him there's going to be a grand opening party for the new management and they'll be handing out Mad Dog 20/20 in the ER."

"I'll tell him it's BYOB and we'll see what he shows up with."

The director laughed. "Big picture stuff, you know? Maybe test the voice activated gizmos before investing who knows what for the whole system. I couldn't even guess at what Med Prompt costs. They're probably a couple hundred dollars each. By the way, True, is the triage charting still auto entering everyone being on dialysis?"

"Last time I checked it still is."

The director groaned. "I'm not trying to brag by saying this, first of all. But I get paid a lot of money by this hospital. Why they pay me I don't know. Because I have spent two hours a day for the last month since we got this new electronic charting system putting addendums on charts to fix the auto entries that the computer thinks are helpful. And my point is I could do something more productive. Use my medical degree and management skills for something less clerical. This hospital gets one malpractice suit for anything, any little thing and they do a chart audit? They're screwed. I can hear the attorney now. Every chart indicates that patients are on dialysis. Apparently this is a computer glitch with their charting system. But ladies and gentleman of the jury, how can we believe anything in the chart if these egregious errors are left to stand? If it wasn't documented it wasn't done. I rest my case."

"Why wouldn't they believe the rest of the chart?" asked True.

"Because of the auto-entries. The triage chart has all these auto-entries that are supposed to save us time and build this great chart that bills well because it covers all the bases. Except it inserts entire sentences that you don't see until the chart is signed. You just see the boxes you click at triage for the review. No active kidney issues. No active neurological issues. When the doc signs off the chart at the end of the case, the computer spits out: maintaining dialysis schedule and patient is fully ambulatory in the room with intact reflexes and sensation. Just yesterday it did that on one of my patients who was a quadriplegic. Do you know I was about to sign a new doc a few months ago who would have been perfect to work here except when he heard we were getting this computer charting system he changed his mind? I thought he was exaggerating, you know? One of those older guys who's not very technologically savvy, can't type, whatever. Oh no. He knew what he was talking about. He'd worked with this system at a different hospital and quit not long after they installed it because it was such a liability quagmire."

"What does the administration say when you point this out?"

"That IT is working on it. I've given up on that. And that we all just need to work harder. That it can't be that bad. That the dialysis mistake had been fixed last week. You know what? The contract is nearly up. I just edit the charts to the extent that I can so that none of them come back to bite us in the ass down the road. At least I don't have nearly as many meetings to go to. It's actually kind of fun being a lame duck administrator."

"Why?" asked True.

"Because my answer to everything is 'Good Luck with that' and that's about it," she said.

"I see your point," True said. Two men were wheeling a cart with orange buckets and some bottled water alongside the desks. They put a five gallon water bottle on top of the cart.

The director glared. "Are we doing this again today?"

The first man smiled nervously. "Just a precaution. If we have to turn off the water it will just be for thirty minutes or so. We'll let you know."

"If you're bringing out the orange buckets to flush the toilets then it's going to happen. You know we're in the midst of a stomach flu outbreak right? Every patient that can get to a toilet is using it ten times while they're here," the director said.

"We know," the man replied.

"Will you at least put signs on the bathrooms to say out of order before you turn the water off?" she asked.

"Don't know if we have those, doc. I'll check."

They left and the director shook her head. She didn't look confident in any signs being found.

"Were you here the other day when they did this? No warning. And enough water for about twenty minutes. Boiler room problem," she shook her head. "Good luck with that. Anyways, the bottom line is the new group coming in is going to get their asses handed to them they will be so understaffed. And I feel for you guys. But not enough to stay."

"Why isn't anybody going to stay?" asked the nurse.

The boss rolled her eyes. "Where to start? Aside from the crappy computer system? Or the fact that at some point today I just know the toilets are going to overflow? It's not you guys. You all are great. No, unfortunately the nurses will be equally screwed over by this. It was an underhanded deal, first of all. No bids. No transparency. Just stone-wall, stone-wall, stone-wall and then surprise, we're canceling your contract. They announced it by email no less."

"What?" said True. "That's weak. That's like breaking up by text."

"I know. OMG, screw you, LOL. How professional. This place is the consolation prize for the other sites the group is taking over. Whatever. Business, right? Corporate consolidation. They wanted all the lucrative suburban sites but they had to take Holy Tino's with it. But then the new group takes this don't call us, we'll call you, send us your cv attitude. Most of us already had offers from other hospitals when these clowns come back with easily the worst offer I have ever seen. A pay cut. Buy your own malpractice insurance. A contract clause that says half your pay is paid quarterly at the discretion of the board? What is that? They want warm bodies to staff this place that's all."

"I bet it goes to pay for the new CEO's botox habit," True added.

"Then it's definitely a losing battle. There is no amount of money in the world that will make that face look good," said the director. "Have you ever been in her office? She has a picture of her two pet mastiffs with those big jowls. Uncanny resemblance."

"I used to work for a coffee shop in college where I got paid by the discretion of the owner," Maglio volunteered. "His checks bounced so he would always pay me in cash out of the till. Don't need to go back to that."

"Is he still in business?" asked the director.

"What do you think," said Maglio.

"They've got to be green at this. Or they don't care who works here. Hmm. Incompetent, underfunded or disingenuous, I'm not sure which to take. Then nobody bites at their crappy offer and they come back with version two that suddenly includes malpractice insurance but oops, now we have to take away the partnership track. We're back to warm bodies. No thanks."

"So who do we get to staff this place when you all leave?"

"New grads, honey. Get ready. Fresh out of residency."

"Oh, God," the nurse said.

"Oh, yes. Doing the mega work up, testing Raymond's blood alcohol level as if it matters, and doling out Percocet to the scammers so they tell all their friends. The waiting room times are going to be six hours."

"You can't go," said the nurse.

"Sorry. We've all been there but you don't fill a place with new grads all at once. The blind leading the blind. I'm headed to St. Pat's, I'm sure they need nurses if you want to get off the sinking ship."

"But this sounds like a set up for failure," the nurse said.

"You know what I think?" the director asked. "If you really want to know what I think, I think there was a directive from somebody to just staff the place for a year or two with warm bodies, don't care how, because they know it's going to close. Just like St. John's."

The nurse frowned. "I used to work at St. John's. Actually I worked there right before it closed. The last year was terrible."

I turned around and Jerry was gone. He had walked over to the mural they were talking about. It ran the length of the entry/

exit hallway and featured a collage of local architecture, birds, and fish. "She is skinny, but not in a bad way," Jerry said, pointing toward the young college kid up on the ladder. "I think True is being a little hard on her."

"I think I'm going with the boss on this one," I said. "Painting a mural seems like a strange priority from what I know about this place. But maybe it's the start of a generalized facelift."

"What do you know? You just died here. When did you ever spend any time here? This place is great. Except it doesn't make any money."

"Jerry, it's the busiest hospital in the city. It's in the news every other week. How can they not make money?"

"Who can pay? How often do suburbanites like you end up here? I would think you would have picked a nicer hospital to go die in. I've heard about this. They all talk, you know? They have a great crew here. They have people who want to be here. This take-over thing. Rumors for a while, you know? And rumors the whole place is going to get shut down. Just like what happened to St. John's a few years ago. Running in the red. Now it's really going to happen. There's not going to be anything in this part of the city for thirty blocks or more. Makes me wonder. They try to run things too lean. That's what's the matter with corporate America these days. This hospital is part of a bigger conglomerate and they keep opening specialty places in the suburbs. Last time I was here, you know what I found out? They were paying one person to draw blood on the night shift. Costs them twelve bucks an hour to have one person. And it was taking forever. So who was drawing the blood? The docs. Costs who knows what per hour."

"Just how much time did you spend here?"

"Hey, I'm an old guy. After my kidneys shut down I hung out here at least three times a week for dialysis and that was when I was feeling good. The other four days a week I ended up here because I felt like crap."

"So you spent every day here."

"Pretty much. These people are family."

"I want to get out of here. Jerry, don't take this the wrong way but I have a family. They're in room 4."

"Still watching the game."

I glared at Jerry. "Everybody handles stress differently. Some people carry on with normal activity."

"What are you, a grief counselor? You better not be one of them. I can't stand them."

"I'm not a grief counselor."

"That's a relief. You know you're missing a real opportunity."

I groaned. "I have no interest in going to the nurses' locker room."

"I'm not talking about that. We can do that later. I'm talking about your family. You should go listen. You'll have had a chance to hear what everyone really thinks about you. If you come back from the dead you might even need to change your will. Who knows?"

"Why do you care?"

"I don't. But I need to have something to do until Dr. Maglio signs my death certificate."

"Look, Jerry. I know you're trying to help. You've been a great host since I showed up. But do me a favor. Just stay out of my business, ok?"

"Touchy, touchy. What did you get your wife for Christmas?" he asked.

"A thing that makes paninis."

"A kitchen thing?"

"Yes, a kitchen thing."

Jerry shook his head. "Did she like it?"

"Of course she did," I said.

"Has she made you any paninis with it yet?"

"Well, no," I said.

Jerry pointed toward room four. "You have work to do if and when you get back. Panini maker. Sheesh. I guarantee if you went in there right now you would find out what she really thought of the panini maker."

I didn't know whether to laugh, cry or hit him. But I knew none of those things would make a difference and I'd never really been in a fight anyway. I didn't want my first fight to be with a dead guy. Of all the damn things to go wrong on a Sunday. On any given Sunday I was not supposed to drop dead. I had so much to live for. And I had only had a first helping of chili when I dropped dead. One great opportunity to eat all the salty snacks or at least hide them under the chili and Laura wouldn't notice, and I blew it by keeling over. And I hadn't even really gotten started on the dips. I would be more balanced when I came back, I thought. Laura could let a bag of chips sit in the pantry for a week and forget about them. I would eat the whole bag in a sitting. Which is why I never bought them. Except when Laura complained that we never had any snacks in the house. So I would go buy them and eat them all anyway. Which led us back to the same place. Our compromise was to not buy them and I would eat my fill outside of the house. Of course in front of other people you can't really eat the whole bag or the whole bowl of artichoke dip. So I moderated myself better in public and then never ate it at home.

"I'm not being touchy, Jerry. I have a lot to live for," I said.

"Like what?"

"My family. My work."

"What do you do since you're not a grief counselor?"

"I'm an accountant."

I must admit the words rang hollow to me as soon as I said them. Just once it would have been nice to have a different answer. Not that it made people run away at cocktail parties. On the contrary I usually ended up trying to avoid the tax questions that inevitably followed. But the world was full of mission statements and position papers. I could probably recite most of Graham and Graham Accounting's mission statement if I had to. Wasn't I supposed to have a bigger reason to live? Some great summary of what was important if only to shut Jerry up for a while? I could have told him I was a secret agent. How would he have known otherwise?

I had my affairs in order, as they say in the business. I had a will, a trust fund for each kid, life insurance, and homeowner's insurance. Laura had been talking about going back to work now that the kids were both out of the house but she wasn't sure where to look first. Both our cars were paid off. It wasn't tax season so work had been actually pleasant for the past few months. Was there more to it? Did I have to bargain in order to come back? I thought about the big ones. World hunger. Cancer. International terrorism. Global warming. I didn't have a clue as to how to tackle any of those. AIDS. The national debt. If this was going to be a test of the worth of Alan Fries CPA, I was going to come up short.

I ran through the checkbook balance. The tuition was paid for this semester. The mortgage payment was sent. I was pretty sure neither car needed an oil change for at least another two months. I started to panic. My checklist had a lot of completes on it. That might not be good.

OK, maybe it's not the global big things. Maybe it's the personal big things. I had never climbed Mt. Everest before. Or the Alps. Or anything higher than 2000 feet, actually. There were limitations to living in the Midwest. Is it still an acceptable bucket list if you add things posthumously? I hadn't checked the mortgage rates lately. Maybe there was a great chance to refinance the house. I could come back and do that. Laura never had a grasp of compound interest.

Jerry was looking at me with a raised, grizzled eyebrow. I think they were raised. It was tough to say for sure as he had so many white bristles standing straight out of his eyebrows it was tough to see his eyes. I noticed the strange looking IV taped to his neck and the large, ropey veins on his forearms. It was hard not to stare.

"For dialysis," he said, answering my unasked questions. "The fistulas in my arms clotted off. They all do eventually. I just got the other line put in my neck."

I grimaced. I had never liked medicine or medical procedures. When I had taken aptitude tests in high school and college, apparently I scored well on reasoning and logic. Somehow this led a guidance counselor to a list of possible career matches. I could understand why doctor and accountant were both on the list; one had to be methodical for both. But if I smelled antiseptic or saw blood or did both at the same time, I usually became so nauseous I had to run. The counselor had "tut-tutted" that worry with a wave of her hand as if it was something I could outgrow. But for me, the career choice was obvious.

Maybe if I came back I could volunteer in the hospital. My stomach turned at the thought. I could help a lot after this. I could talk with people about to undergo unpleasant experiences like bladder catheters. I could use the experience for good. Unless I vomited in front of the person. Which I thought I might do now. I couldn't help staring at the dialysis catheter and was feeling squeamish. I had never been a good vomiter. Which probably saved me from becoming the alcoholic that some of my college friends had become. They could drink and drink and reach that certain point, vomit, and then carry on as if the party had never stopped. Me, I would drink and drink, reach that certain point and feel so nauseous for the next seventeen hours that I wanted to die and then I finally would vomit. And then I would only feel well enough to consider leaving the bathroom for my bed. So I never became much of a drinker.

"Do you think we have a destiny? Do you think once we fulfill it we die? I can't imagine I've done what I was supposed to get done on earth."

"Fifty-two years wasn't enough time to get something done? You must be quite a procrastinator. Do you think bargaining actually works?" Jerry replied.

"Hey, it's worth a try. I must be here for a reason. I could be a volunteer in the hospital."

"Must there be a reason? You think God will bring you back so that you can minister to people afraid of getting a garden hose up the schlong? A cosmic reason would be nice wouldn't it? Except I don't want a cosmic reason for why my wife died ten years before me, and why I got cancer. That would make God look like kind of a jerk, right?"

"But you lived a long life. Longer than me if I don't get out of this," I said.

"Does that mean God likes me better than you?"

"Jerry, it's not that simple."

"Does he like me better than my wife? If he does then he's really a screwball because my wife was a peach. She did a lot for the neighbors, everybody knew her. I haven't done much in the last ten years other than be an IV crash test dummy for nurses and doctors in training."

"It's not like that. You're over simplifying things."

"Well, Cheese, I agree with you there. It's certainly not as simple as you tell the big guy you decided you want to have a crack at ending world hunger so would he be so kind as to bring you back to life and the comforts of your suburban home and, poof, there you are."

"That's not what I'm asking for."

"It isn't? It sure sounds like it," said Jerry.

"I don't know what I'm asking for. But I want to live and I don't want to stay here."

"So you're trying to apply your case as being unique so that you'll get to come back. You know, Alan, a lot of talented people die when they don't want to. And, I'm not particularly talented, but as you have pointed out, I lived longer than you. Even if you have some talent, are you better than Mozart? Better than Elvis?"

"That is not a fair comparison. They both died through excess. Elvis passed out drunk in a plate of mashed potatoes and didn't Mozart catch syphilis? I don't have any of their vices. I'm not counting accidents either. That skews the numbers."

"I had a few vices and I still lived longer than you. Except the syphilis part. I never had that. Not sure if Mozart did either. I think he passed out drunk in some plate of something too. I even lived longer than one of my doctors. Guy was out on a motorcycle and hits a deer. Big neck injury. Gone in an instant. That was twenty years ago. Besides, you're only half dead really. So look on the bright side and don't be so gloomy. It looks like they're taking you up to intensive care. Do you want to follow along?"

I watched the bed roll slowly out of room 4 with the attendant IV poles, ventilator, and a small army of medical staff. I shook my head. I wasn't sure where I wanted to go, but I didn't want to go there. If I just stayed calm, I would feel it any moment. An inverse of one of those falling dreams where your body jerks awake at the last second. And I would be back in my skin. It seemed likely. I felt alive. I hadn't had any of those visions you hear about, like going toward a light or walking up a staircase. It had to be just a matter of time before this would be resolved.

It wasn't fair. I thought it and felt it with every fiber I had and yet it sounded so juvenile. Of course it wasn't fair. Tell that to the other poor bastards that wind up in that room. But I didn't understand Jerry. I wasn't sure I wanted to but so far he was the only person I could talk to so I might as well try to understand him. He wasn't railing against death. He seemed so laissez-faire. How was he ready for it? I didn't think I would be ready for it at eighty-seven. It wouldn't matter what age. I would be terrified. I was terrified now.

    I had been methodical. I took vitamins, took a cholesterol lowering pill, ate garlic, ran on the treadmill three times a week and had even tried yoga, well once I tried yoga. The women made me nervous in the class. It wasn't just that they were gorgeous, which made me embarrassed. It was that they were aggressively gorgeous, balancing on one hand and staring ahead while I vainly tried to touch my toes without throwing out my back permanently. They talked about chakras and auras and cleansing diets. They took herbal this and that and their skin glowed in the hot room. I learned later that the instructor turned the temperature up on purpose allegedly to help everyone's muscles loosen up. It just made me sweat more and turn red. I didn't glow when I exercised. You try sitting at a desk during tax season for sixteen hours straight. Yoga is not what is needed after that. Maybe a chiropractor or the jaws of life. Just to be able to stand up and get out of the chair.

    Laura had been going to yoga though. When our youngest headed to college last fall, she started different classes at the Y under the pretext of going back to work. She never balanced on one hand or stood on her head when I was around. But she came home humming a melody I couldn't recognize. I thought about what Jerry said about my friend ogling her. That was ridiculous. Laura was nice enough looking but for ogling?

    What if it was true? Maybe she poisoned me. Maybe Kevin poisoned me. Laura knew a lot about herbal tea. And she had been buying the herbal medicinal kinds of tea. She had even brought a box home for me that was supposed to have male "balancing" effects. It tasted like soap and she hadn't been very pleased when I had said that. And then when I poured it in the sink and only thought to ask afterwards if she wanted it. She had sniffed at me and reminded me that it was a male "balancing" tea and she shouldn't drink it. She had her own brand, or concoction, or whatever you called it. It came in a box with soothing pastel colors and pictures of bamboo and flying cranes. Mine came in a dark green box with a picture of a dragon in front of a mountain. I had told her that most of it was just packaging and placebo and she hadn't been happy about that either. She knew a lot about herbicides too. That wasn't much of a stretch, was it? Ever since she became devoted to organic gardening she began studying the side effects of herbicides. She told me they were made out of the same ingredients as chemical weapons.

Of course she hadn't poisoned me.

It would have gone against her principles. And we had a good marriage. It was my first, her second and last, as she took great pains to remind me. Her first husband had been far more volatile. They married young, only lasted three years, and had one kid, a daughter. She had kicked him out and kept the house. Not long after that the idiot had dumped lawn fertilizer and de-icing agents all over her tomato beds one afternoon when she wasn't home. She came home and saw the green pellets and salt clumps everywhere and went and knocked on her neighbors' doors. They happened to have seen him in the yard, why yes, they didn't think anything of it at the time.

She went to his office and in the midst of a sea of cubicles called him a pathetic Minnesota house-wife who couldn't stand the fact that some missus up the road was going to win the biggest cucumber contest at the state fair. As we were already dating at the time I took that as a roundabout compliment on my manhood. God, I missed her.

I could take her to Cuba. I heard you could get there even if you were an American if you didn't fly directly from the US. I could surprise her with a trip. Except we would need to get a lot of vaccinations before we left. She might wonder why I was scheduling appointments for yellow fever and hepatitis shots for both of us. I could tell her it was like going for a couples massage only less naked. She had sprung one of those on me when we went to Hilton Head over Labor Day weekend one year. She kept laughing because I didn't know why I was waiting in the salon with her when the hotel room had a great big screen TV. And then a young man and woman came out from the hall dressed in gym-teacher clothing and told us to follow them. They weren't at all sexy, thank God. They were efficient. They told us to get undressed and put towels over our nethers and lay down on the two tables and then they left the room. I may sound a little slow but it wasn't until that point that it dawned on me what I was in for.

"Who massages who?" I asked Laura in a whisper.

"I think the girl does you and the guy does me," she replied.

"Does me?" I had asked. That had a certain connotation and I hoped Laura hadn't paid for the happy ending. I had never had a professional massage before but I had heard stories from friends in college.

"Massages you," Laura said, rolling her eyes.

The young woman who did me kept telling me to relax. I don't know if it worked but I finally left the salon or clinic or whatever they call those places feeling, if not relaxed, then at least very tired. And I smelled like the geranium oil my grandmother sprayed on me when we visited. She told me it kept away mosquitoes. It didn't keep away other neighborhood kids because they told me I smelled like flowers and then they called their friends to come smell me. It usually ended up in a shoving match at best and a fistfight at worst. That was one of the reasons I didn't like to visit my grandparents in the summer.

Chapter 3

I settled into the chair by the radiology station while Jerry made his way back into room 4. There was a very loud guy who by the sounds of it had been shot. And he was hell bent on getting patched up so he could head back out to the street to shoot the guy back. I wasn't in the mood for watching that. I was trying not to think about what might be wrong with my disconnected body. True and Dr. Maglio were talking about her kids.

"I'm not sure what to do with Max," she said.

"Why?"

"Well, I thought he made a breakthrough. He's eleven, you know. Can't get the kid to bathe. He hates showers, hates baths. He's right at that age where he seriously needs to start using deodorant and he never remembers to. But the other day he came home from school and asked me for help."

"With deodorant?"

"No, with a girl. He decided he liked a girl in his class and he wanted to ask her out."

"At eleven? That's a fast mover."

"I told him he could go to a movie with her but only if I drove and sat behind them."

"Sounds like a great date."

"Hey, you're the one who pointed out he's eleven. But I was going along with it because he said he wanted to smell good when he asked her out," True said.

"So far Max sounds like a normal evolving male."

"And he wanted my advice on what to wear when he talked to her."

"He wants his mother to dress him? OK, he's not sounding like a normal evolving male anymore."

"Can you just listen, Maglio, without editorializing every five seconds? So I bought him some body wash for the shower and new deodorant and helped him pick out a nice shirt and pants. We're doing all this the night before school mind you. He can be very methodical when he cares about something you know. And then the next morning he takes a shower and uses the body wash and everything and comes down to breakfast early. I mean, if Max did this on exam days he would be golden."

They were interrupted by a patient singing loudly on a gurney as he was wheeled past.

Maglio raised an eyebrow. "Hey buddy. Are you Raymond Ray?"

"All day long, brother."

"OK, True, I know that guy. I had to check. So Max has the smell good on and he's ready for school."

True called to the nurse assigned to Raymond's room. "Donna, will you get him a urinal before it's too late."

Donna muttered something back and stomped to the supply closet.

"Where was I? Right, so he's ready. He's going to ask her at recess. And I'm post nights so I go to sleep as soon as he heads to school. He comes home on the bus that afternoon and absolutely will not talk about it. Zip. He goes into the bathroom and I hear water running so I think, wow, two showers in one day. This is going to be great."

Donna passed by and gave True a withering look. "And you were too busy to bring him a urinal? Thanks a lot. Do you know how bad it smells in that room already?"

"Hey, I'm getting advice from Maglio here. I need a male opinion and I'm not going to bother with one from my ex," said True. "Besides, it would smell worse if he didn't get the urinal."

"I'm going on break," said Donna, already pulling her cigarette pack out of her scrub pocket. "I told my nursing student to come get you if my patients need anything. Like their urinals emptied."

"So anyway," True returned to Dr. Maglio. "Max finally comes out of the bathroom, goes to his room and comes out much later dressed in the same pajamas he's had for at least a week. He comes into the kitchen and tells me 'It didn't go well,' and I ask him what he means. Apparently the girl told him that she's only eleven and she's not allowed to go out with boys."

"At least somebody has smart parents."

"Screw you, Maglio. I told you I was just going along with it because he wanted to bathe. I thought it was a good incentive. But then he tells me that he took another shower to wash off all that flowery smelling stuff and to get rid of the deodorant smell. Is this normal? I look at Raymond and I have to think he was a cute kid somewhere along the line," said True.

"Until he got permanently drunk and lost his marbles? If you're asking me whether Max is going to ever bathe again I think he probably will. I think it took more than a rejection at eleven to screw up Raymond."

"But he wasn't exactly rejected. She isn't allowed. There's a difference."

"That's like what an adult says when they're too busy at work. It's just using the corporation as an excuse. He got rejected. He'll get over it."

We all want the best for our kids, I thought. Trite but true. My kids were on their own at college, whether I was dead or not, they had built whatever character they were going to build. Laura's daughter had a five year old in kindergarten this year. I had to remember that I was a grandfather. I glanced sideways at Jerry. Best not to talk about it around him. I wouldn't hear the end of it. But Clare had turned five this year and her mother had enrolled her in a private kindergarten that garnered all sorts of accolades in the press. From what I had seen, most of the accolades should have come from marketing. Our information had been given to the registrar ostensibly for special events at the school but the fundraising blitz was continual. It was a k12 program so the little geniuses would all be matriculating into the upper grades if their parents could keep coughing up the tuition so maybe some of the upgrades to the campus were needed. But the kindergarten playground was already state of the art as far as those things went and the teachers all made their own play dough out of organic flour and beet roots. That's what they told us at least. I couldn't see where the extra fundraising was going. The fundraising pitches came in two forms, either an invitation to the school to attend some big ticket event that was inevitably described as "fabulous" or a guilt trip on how little Susie from across the tracks would be doomed to public school and early pregnancy but for the generous scholarship funds provided by people who were already coughing up full tuition. As the grandparents we were considered the prime source of the trust fund apparently.

    Look if I sound bitter it's because Laura's daughter has received a lot of help from us over the last ten years and I don't quite know where it's gone. And when I think about how long it took me to pay back the loans needed to get my degree and accounting certificate, the rationale to pay college tuition for a kindergarten is a little far-fetched. I picked up Clare the other week as a favor and I thought I was at the UN. The phalanx of black sport utility vehicles stretched around the traffic circle and every parent had a neon dashboard sign with their kid's name on it. The teachers walked the little kids to the cars, heaved them into the back seats, and the phalanx lurched forward another ten feet. The drivers all drove horribly slowly and waited until the kid had seven seatbelts on and maybe a crash helmet before they moved. It was painful. Every once in a while some mom got impatient and would try to cut in line which threw the whole procession of SUVs into a panic because then nobody would let her in but she managed to block two lanes for the twenty minutes it took to correct the lumbering trajectory of the vehicle. One may as well have tried to change lanes in a shipping canal.

Maybe if I had had the right start in kindergarten I wouldn't have died watching the Bears-Vikings game. I should have been a big donor to the school. I grimaced; that would have been worse. That would have guaranteed an early demise. Some successful guy who is furthering a great cause by helping inner-city kids attend Mount Muckedty-Muck Academy gets some tragic terminal disease, lingers on just long enough to "fight it" and then dies in time for the autumn alumnae magazine to have a big obituary. What a cliché. No, that would definitely have clinched it. At least ventricular fibrillation hadn't been painful.

I looked up into the ER, suddenly realizing I had been holding my head in my hands. The place was making me paranoid.

"The thing with Max is, he's too smart for his own good," True said to Dr. Maglio.

Maglio raised one eyebrow. "Doesn't every parent say that?"

"Probably. But he was sent to detention last week for talking or something and he came home and was so happy."

"Proud he went to detention?"

"No, but he said he liked detention. It was quiet, he got all his homework done and now he could relax at home and by the way, could he watch TV. was what he said. He wants to go to detention every day now."

"Other kids accomplish that by going to library after school to get their homework done. Or study hall. Don't they have study hall anymore?"

"Study hall is punitive. The library is loud. He's just a kid who doesn't want to take work home with him. Who can blame him? He's got this innate sense of work-life balance. He's brilliant. He got more done in detention than he ever gets done at home."

"It sounds like he's scammed you into sympathy with a new twist on the ancient truth that True, no kid likes homework."

True sighed. "You think I'm too easy on him?"

"Duh," said Maglio.

"You should have seen it though. He got everything done. And I think he got it right."

"Wait a minute, True. He's how old? You 'think' he got it right."

"That's easy for you to say. When was the last time you needed to know state capitals?"

I hadn't been easy on my kids. Laura hadn't been easy on them. Her daughter, yes, but our two kids together, they had a good foundation. All the structured activities had abated of course, as they headed off to college. I had helped them with math homework. Laura had helped with other projects and essays. There had been some halcyon days, now that I looked back at it. I never knew the state capitals but that's what flashcards were for. I might slow down my work schedule now that they were older. Take some time for myself. Recover from my near death experience.

A young man walked up to Dr. Maglio and True carrying a brown paper bag stuffed with clothes. It was the same guy who had bagged up my pens, cell phone and wallet.

"Where are they doing the clothing collection for the homeless?" he asked.

"In the closet next to the decon room. Alvarez, is that your sweater?" True reached into the bag and pulled out a brown, paisley, wool item shot through with shiny gold stripes.

"Only briefly. Now it's going to Goodwill."

"This was your sweater? This looks like Liberace took Dr. Huxtable shopping. And it has three quarter length sleeves. This is a woman's sweater. Did you actually buy this?"

Alvarez sighed. "No, I didn't buy it. But you might look good in it. It was a Christmas present from my sister."

"I'm speechless. Does she know that you're straight?"

"Hostile work environment. I don't have to answer that."

"Are you straight?" True asked.

Alvarez glared at her.

True rifled through the bag. She pulled out a camouflage sweatshirt. "Are you allowed to give away your army stuff if you're still in the reserves?"

"Why, do you want that too?" Alvarez asked.

"Not really. And I don't want the first one either. But if you have a picture of you wearing it I'd love that. Because I'll hang it up in the break room."

"Not going to happen. The camo sweatshirt was from my brother. It's not army issue."

"Because he figures somebody in the army doesn't have enough camo already?" True snorted.

"It's the thought that counts, right? It's not like I need clothes anyways."

"I don't know. Straight to goodwill seems worse than re-gifting," Maglio chimed in. "Don't you at least have to wear it to a family function so they can see you in it?"

"Maybe if you're ten years old. I think I had a few itchy sweaters I hated that I had to wear to make Grandma happy. But these days? The next family function won't be until next Christmas with the schedules we have here. Somebody can use this stuff, its cold out there." Alvarez stuffed the clothes back in the bag.

"But that's how you know your family loves you. When you work the night shift and they celebrate Christmas at 2pm on the 28th of December," said Maglio.

"And you return the love by putting their sweaters in the goodwill," said True.

"I'll pass on the guilt, thank you very much," said Alvarez. "Remember. I just had Christmas dinner with my mother. Big helpings of guilt. Someone will love these sweaters. Maybe someone color blind."

"You're sure you want to put that gold lame' one in the bin? It's unique. What if your sister is downtown and runs into some crazy guy talking to parking meters wearing her gift to you?"

"Small chance. She might be the one talking to the parking meters depending what she's on that day."

"Is she using again?" asked True.

Alvarez frowned. "Actually, I don't think so. Nothing major anyway. I think she's getting back into the shit slowly and thinks she can control it this time. My mom still pretends it never happened. And then they sit together and talk about how hard life is and how my sister still can't get a job. The last place fired her because she wouldn't do a drug test after an on the job injury. She 'forgot' to report the injury for a week and then tried to get it covered. Basic, right? I'm just a security guard, you know. I'm not some criminal attorney. But if you sign the forms when they hire you, you know it's going to happen at some point, right? Either your job is more important than whatever you smoke or it's not and you piss hot. Not according to my mother. No, Denise was fired out of the clear blue through no fault of her own."

"Your mom probably knows the truth but doesn't want to talk about it in front of you," True said.

"I don't want to talk about it either. But I'm tired of coming home to hear what a great success it is that Denise got out of bed today and made it to the Christmas party when I spent the last week working double shifts just to get some time off to come to the party."

The secretary was on the phone again. "I remember you, sir. Yes, you called earlier. No, we haven't found them yet. You put them in a cup when you had your x-rays, I understand. Yes, I asked them if they had seen them. No, I didn't personally look for them. I need to stay at this desk to answer the phone. So I can talk to you when you call. You may have to take this up further with the hospital if it is that important to you. I'm sure they're very nice. Don't raise your voice at me. Son of a bitch, he hung up on me."

Alvarez frowned. "What was that all about?"

"Some guy lost his nipple rings here when he went to x-ray. That's about the fifth time he's called to see if we found them."

Alvarez shook his head. "I don't get it. I would be too embarrassed to call and talk to a complete stranger about something like that. And no, I don't have any," he added pointedly as he looked at Maglio. "If I did and I lost them, I would just consider them lost."

"What if it was your good pair?" asked True.

"My what?"

"Your good pair. Some of those are really expensive."

"I don't need to know that," said Alvarez.

"Do you want me to give the sweater to Raymond the next time he needs one?" Maglio asked.

"Doc, if you do, I don't even want to know either." Alvarez turned and carried the bag toward the decontamination room.

Maglio laughed. "So why do we still care what we get for Christmas? We're adults, right? It shouldn't matter."

"It does and it doesn't," said True.

"That's deep," said Maglio.

"It doesn't have to be the perfect present but it should be something at least relevant."

"I give everybody the same thing each year. I go to one place and get a case of wine and everybody gets a bottle. The next year, I'll go to the coffee place and everybody gets a pound of whole beans."

"But what if they don't drink?"

"Don't care."

"What if they're a recovering alcoholic?"

"Then they should know better and they can regift it to someone else."

"What if they don't have a coffee bean grinder?"

"Then they should join civilization and go get one."

"What if they're children?"

Maglio paused and thought for a moment. "You got me there. Usually it's a gift card then to one of those kids' stores. My wife handles that part."

"You'd really give your best friend a bag of coffee beans for Christmas?" True asked.

"My best friends know not to expect anything from me for Christmas. Christmas is for the obligation presents. Kids are the exception. They're probably fun to shop for. I wouldn't know. Friends don't get obligation presents. You do things with your friends because you want to. Throughout the year. You do things with your family on Christmas because you think you have to. It's a ritual. It doesn't matter what's in the box. I bet Alvarez gave his sister that sweater last year and just forgot about it."

True raised an eyebrow at him.

"OK, maybe not. But you get my point."

"I hope you work every Christmas so that your less bah-humbugged colleagues can enjoy the day."

"Usually," Maglio smirked.

"Ugh," said True.

"This year we went out of town."

"You and your wife went out of town for Christmas?" True was incredulous.

"We went to the Bahamas."

"Alone? No other family?"

"It was beautiful. I think my wife felt a little guilty. She told her relatives that my side of the family was having a reunion over the holidays and it was a destination. They don't usually cross paths but you never know."

"No tree? No presents?"

"A palm tree. Actually a few of those. And we exchanged presents. I think I gave everyone else bottles of olive oil from the organic place my wife goes to. I can't remember."

"You can't remember what you gave people for Christmas? Maglio, it was barely last week. What is wrong with you?"

"My dog gave me the best present this year," said Maglio.

"I don't think I want to hear this," said True.

"No, really, he did. I thought I was going to have to take him to the vet for a bowel obstruction surgery but it worked itself out. You know those little white wrappers that come inside the lid of a French onion dip container? Not the hard plastic but the flexible plastic liner that you have to peel off after you take off the lid? There's still a lot of dip on there and Dingus loves cheese. He inhaled it right off the coffee table and swallowed it in a second. I was sure that would cause a blockage somewhere.

But a couple days later, we're out for a walk and he stops to do his thing and I see this white thing coming out. It was horrible. I thought he had a tapeworm. And he's straining a bit and then it's out. The plastic had kind of formed itself into a tube. It looked like a chocolate cannoli."

"That's it," said True. "Dinner and delivery is on you tonight and we are getting Italian food."

"Deal. It wasn't as bad as when he ate mouse poison."

"Mouse poison?"

"He was digging up the yard last summer like crazy. We had a pest control guy come out and put these fake boulder mouse traps out. They are supposed to be completely impenetrable to dogs.

No dog has ever gotten into one. No worries. So I have a day off and the afternoon rolls around and I head outside to have a beer, sit in the yard, maybe even throw a ball for the damn thing, and all over the yard are little blue pellets and the mouse trap fake rock is flipped over and the inner chamber thing is half chewed and there next to the dog is a dead mouse and a dead chipmunk. I think he was trying to rescue them.

Anyways, I called the animal poison control number. Did you know they have a separate one? My wife has an emergency binder for the dog, she's that organized. Costs fifty bucks just to talk to someone on this line, they bill your phone directly, shows up on your phone bill. Unbelievable. We have to go get hydrogen peroxide, give him some to induce vomiting and then we spent the next hour watching the poor guy throw up all over the driveway and I'm poking at the vomit with a stick to see if there are any blue pellets in there. Nothing. We're in the clear. I call back the poison control and they tell me that dogs have a different shaped stomach than people and even though we didn't see blue pellets, we still need to take him to the vet for an antidote. Well, why did you make me give the dog crap to make him throw up all over the driveway then? Do you know what she told me? As a precaution. As a precaution for what? Couldn't answer that." Maglio picked up the death paperwork on Jerry, frowned, and put it back down.

"When was this?"

"Last summer. On my day off. I mentioned that right? On my day off."

"You act like you only had one day off for the whole summer."

"I think that's all I had. We hadn't hired the new guy yet."

"Dr. McCallister?"

"Him. The one who calls in sick all the time."

"I think you're exaggerating."

"About McCallister calling in sick?"

"No, about having only one day off for the summer."

"Oh. Anyways, it wasn't that bad. I didn't shoot the dog."

"I bet you would shoot your own dog."

"Tempting," Maglio said. "My wife is one of those dog philosophers, thinks dogs are smarter than people and that they have these deep insights into your moods. She told me that the dog was here to teach us something."

"What did you say?"

"I told her the dog was here to teach us marksmanship after he chewed up six feet of cedar siding from the house."

"Are you guys ever going to have kids?" True asked.

Maglio chuckled. "Your timing is great. I can almost confidently say never."

"Almost?"

He leaned in towards her. "Vasectomy."

"No way."

"Recovering. Remember when I took a few days off and came back limping and pissed off?"

"When are you not pissed off at work?"

"Good point. Anyways I was limping, limping with both legs and that's not easy to do. It hurt like hell. But that was a month ago and today is the day I drop off my first sample."

True frowned for a moment. "Are you talking about what I think you're talking about?"

"Shooting blanks is the goal. They check two samples to confirm it post op."

"You're dropping it off today? Like you have it with you?" True looked under the desk and behind her as if the offending substance might be right there.

"Relax. It's in the fridge."

"Oh for God's sake, Maglio. People put food in there."

"They shouldn't. Have you seen the inside of it?" he asked.

"Not lately. I keep my lunch in my purse. But some people put food in there."

"And don't take it out for three weeks which is why that fridge is the way it is. But, if it's any consolation, it's in a Genius Bagel's bag."

"That's just wrong. What if it spills?"

"It won't spill. It's in a specimen cup."

True thought for a moment and then got a horrified look on her face. "You didn't produce it here did you?"

Maglio laughed. "Come on, I have some standards. Besides, the shifts are too busy. I don't believe in quickies. I brought it from home and I'm going to run by the clinic this afternoon."

"I hope you grab the wrong bag and bring stale bagels instead."

"As long as there's no sperm in the schmear."

"Gross. What do you have against kids, anyways?"

"Nothing."

"Who's going to take care of you when you're old?"

"The hot nurse I can afford because I didn't spend all my money on kids."

"You won't be able to get it up then anyways."

"I'm a romantic. Ask my wife. It's not all about getting it up."

Two voices from behind the curtain in room 17 were rising. It sounded like the director.

"I don't have to touch your arm."

"All I said was that if you touched my arm I would punch you. But it's a reflex. It hurts. I got in trouble for punching a doctor before so now I tell everyone."

"That's fine, ma'am. Like I said, I don't need to touch your arm. I'm going to go look at your x-rays and then I'll be back."

"But you can touch my arm if he holds my hand."

Another voice chimed in, this one male, volume rising. "I can hold her hand."

"I don't need to touch your arm."

"But that's where it hurts. What if it's broken and it doesn't show up on the x-ray? Can't that happen? You need to touch my arm. And I need some pain meds."

"I'm not going to touch your arm when you threatened to punch me."

"But I won't punch you if he holds my hand."

"Don't worry, I'm here baby. I'll hold your hand," said the male voice.

"I'll be back after I see your x-ray."

It was the director. She sat down and shook her head.

"Don't you have an x-ray to look at?" asked Maglio, grinning.

"That was the most instantaneously passive-aggressive bizarro interaction I have had all week. And she brought her boyfriend along to hold her other arm so she won't punch people. Do you know her? She's the one who used to always come in with the supposed cat bites when she'd been skin popping to get some antibiotics?" She had one of the interns in tow from my resuscitation.

"But you need antibiotics for a cat bite," said the intern, proud of his knowledge.

"That's true, Olson. You also need them for the abscesses that develop from injecting heroin subcutaneously. Cat bites were her cover story."

Olson nodded.

"Anyway, I don't get it. I need to go see someone normal before I look at her x-ray. Therapeutic wait. Maybe she won't come back," the director said.

"Customer service," chided Maglio.

"Don't care. New group. Although I could always tell her the place is about to be under new management and maybe she'll haunt them too. I just don't know how they think this hospital will stay open. The people in this part of Chicago are running out of options."

"Cat bites," Maglio said, lost in thought. "Is she the one that brought in the box wine in her coat and kept asking for more juice that one time we kept her for IV antibiotics? She was making sangria back in room 24."

"Probably," the director said. "That sounds like her."

"How come nobody noticed?" asked Olson.

"We noticed eventually. Busy night. Back room," said Maglio.

True interrupted. "Did you have to fill out a profile for the vasectomy?"

"A profile?" Maglio asked.

"You got a vasectomy?" the director asked.

"A profile. Like a psychological profile to see if you were in the right frame of mind to make the decision. You have to be certain age too, right? They won't do it to a twenty year old."

"I would have filled it out for him," said the director. "Maglio is the perfect candidate for a vasectomy. Not as good as some of our patients, but all the same…"

Sangria. That was a classy drink. Well, not out of a box in the back room in the ER. But done right, that would be a hit at a summer party. A few months to get my strength back and I would roll into summer ready to host the neighbors on the deck. We could even splurge and get a new grill, or a whole outdoor kitchen. Or at least an outlet for the Panini maker. I knew Laura liked her gift, whatever Jerry's opinion of it might be.

Of course I would need to restain the deck. I put it off last season and really shouldn't have. And maybe I would surprise Laura with some of those planter boxes that hung over the deck railing. As long as I padded the railings first so the new stain wouldn't get scraped by the planter boxes. And put some drainage hoses in so they wouldn't drip on the deck when she watered them. That had been why I didn't want them in the first place. But we could plant herbs in them and have fresh basil on whatever we cooked on the new grill. Definitely needed a new grill. I would be done with whatever rehabilitation I needed by then. What was I thinking? That wasn't a reason to come back for. Maybe I could host a charity event and cook on the new grill. Cheeseburgers for cancer research. Would that spoil everyone's appetite and make them think about the carcinogens in charcoal too much? I had never been much of a party thrower. That would have to change. But in the meantime, could I drink wine since I was dead? Was that a part of heaven? I didn't feel much of anything from my body. It was there, I could see its shimmering ghostly outline around my usual frame, but as far as a sense of hunger or thirst, none to be had.

True was washing her hands under the sign that instructed medical professionals how to wash their hands. I was amazed. If I thought the productivity reminders at Graham and Graham were bad, at least they didn't tell me to "rubs hands together for as long as it takes to sing 'happy birthday' using warm but not hot water." She waved her hands under the motion detector and the towel dispenser spit out a towel. I watched the water spin down the drain. We had had a good Christmas, I thought. It had been busy. I waved my hands under the motion detector. Nothing. I looked around for Jerry. He was looking over the intern's shoulder, watching him play games on his phone. I tried again. Still nothing. It was my first day beholden to ghost physics so maybe I was missing something. Why could I pick up objects but not activate the towel dispenser?

True dried her hands efficiently. She had muscular forearms and one had a battle ax tattoo, the other had a flower, I couldn't tell what kind. I think they suited her. Even with the earrings that went up the whole length of her ears, she was attractive. Women like that used to intimidate me and I was never sure why. It wasn't like I had been beaten up by a punk girl or anything. When I came back from this I would strike up a conversation with the first tattooed, pierced person I ran into on the train.

I would share a bottle of wine with Laura when I came back too. She might wear the holiday sweater I had given her for last Christmas. We would sit in the chairs by the fireplace. I couldn't think of when the last time we had done that. Of course I would need to have the chimney cleaned first. And a new chimney cap was in order, not to mention taking the shop vac to the basement clean out. I had told Laura that I was waiting for a humid day to clean it so the dust would settle but the truth was, the shop vac had gotten clogged on something and I didn't know how to fix it. What I really needed was time to smuggle the shop vac to the repair shop without her noticing. I didn't want her to think I was the sort of man who couldn't fix his own shop vac. But after that we would sit by the fireplace and have a glass of wine together.

They had those chimney fire extinguishers. I had seen an ad for one on the in flight magazine the last time Graham and Graham sent me to the CPA conference in Boston. It asphyxiated the fire. The concept was fascinating. Just aim it into the chimney and reverse-squirt. This assumed one thing that I didn't quite understand, namely the ability to stick one's arm into a raging chimney fire and pull a pin. They probably tended to discharge in the living room instead, at which point the person playing hero would be asphyxiated. Now that would have been a better way to die. And imagine the product liability law suit. Laura and the kids would have been in clover.

Had I known that today was to be my day I would have thought this out a little better. Of course it would have still come as a shock. The grim reaper knocking at the door, I might have passed out. But I'm sure if the situation had been explained clearly to me, I would have picked a more financially advantageous way to go. There were enough city buses in Chicago. Hit by a bus, no, hit by a bus while saving a kid who had darted into the road. That would have been noble.

Chapter 4

A man shouted from across the arena. I looked up to watch True attempt to push Raymond in a wheelchair. He had leaned forward and put his arms through the wheels to keep them from turning. True pushed from behind and managed to inch the chair forward a few inches. The rubber wheels squeaked in complaint as they slid across the floor in slow motion. He started to lean forward and she reached around and put her arm across his throat.

"For God's sake, Raymond, you're going to fall on your face and break your arms off in the spokes. We just want to wheel you out so you can wait in the waiting room. We need the beds back here."

"For who? You got some VIP? I want my room back."

"It's not your room."

"Ain' t nobody in the waiting room that needs that room."

The two cops from the other side of the ER saw the struggle and walked over.

"Hey guys, a little help would be great," said True.

The first cop took out his taser.

"You idiot, don't tase him while I have him in a headlock."

The cop seemed to think about it for a moment and then realization spread slowly across his face.

"Just help me push."

Maglio wasn't helping either. He had one eye on the radiology computer and turned his head occasionally to watch True's progress.

"Wang, wang, wang," he said.

Now he had my attention.

"Was it Kim Wang or Mai Wang? Damn. Every time I go to look up an x-ray I forget the patient's name after I sit down. There must be a dozen Wangs that came through today."

"You went through a dozen wangs?" asked Alvarez. The cops had finally pried Raymond's arms out of the wheels and he was grudgingly rolling through the exit doors. I didn't see any gold lame' or paisley patterns but he was wrapped in an enormous coat. I wondered if he appreciated the mural on his way past. I don't think the painter noticed the yelling right below her. The headphone volume would cause hearing loss if she kept it up, I thought. Someone should tell her.

"Very funny. No, I'm looking for Mai Wang. Actually Mai Wang's x-ray. Her x-ray."

"You named your wang after a girl? That's a little weird, man."

"Why don't you go look for someone else's wang so I can get some work done. There's a guy in room 18 with priapism," said Maglio.

"What the heck is priapism?" asked Alvarez.

"Its what the Viagra commercials warn you about. You end up in the ER and somebody like Maglio has to drain the blood out with needles and IV tubing." True was back from depositing Raymond in the waiting room and did not look very pleased with Alvarez and his lack of help. She did, however, seem to be enjoying watching the color drain from his face.

"That's messed up. I don't know how anybody could go through medical school if you have to do things like that," said Alvarez, shaking his head.

"I'd do it for you. If it would save your wang," said Maglio, still scrolling through the xrays on the computer screen. "That's what I took the Hippocratic oath for. I'm a wang saver. On days when I'm not much of a life saver."

"Do you think that guy that we ice-packed is going to make it?" True asked.

"The one with the football fans for a family? He might. He got the right treatments. But you never know. He might wake up a vegetable."

Alvarez frowned. "I thought if you're a vegetable you don't wake up."

"It's a technical thing. More complicated than wang saving. Raymond left before we could give him a new sweater, by the way. True kicked him out."

"He doesn't need a sweater. The man needs some common sense and a cup of coffee," said Alvarez. "He probably had a few blankets stuffed under his coat anyways. He usually does."

"Common sense is not too common. I've seen his head CT, you know. I scanned him the last time he fell down drunk and he has the most atrophy I think I've ever seen on a drunk. Alcohol has not been kind to his brain. I fear for the future, you know?" said Maglio. "We have this entire society that supposed to be investing and doing the 401K thing and living the free market dream. This guy a couple days ago came in as a possible suicide attempt. He'd told his roommate or girlfriend or somebody that he'd taken a bunch of pills to try to kill himself. I go talk to him and he's a regular pill user. Percocet, darvocet, whatever he can get, he takes about twenty pills a day for fun. Swallows some, snorts some. Twenty-two years old. No job. Gets disability payments for chronic something or other. Anyway, I asked him how many pills he took in this overdose attempt because he seems wide awake to me. He tells me he took five or six pills. I had to ask him to repeat himself. How many do you normally take to get high? Twenty. How many did you take in this overdose attempt? Five," Maglio banged his fist on the counter and the radiology computer screen fizzled, temporarily blacking out the Wangs that Maglio was scanning.

Alvarez frowned. "That wouldn't be enough to overdose, would it?"

"Exactly!" Maglio shouted. "This guy didn't even have the basic math skills to kill himself. I was about to explain it to him but then I thought that might incriminate me. He was basically saved by his inability to do math. And don't take this the wrong way, I don't think he was really suicidal. I think he just wanted attention.

So don't think I'm that calloused, OK? But when I walked out the room, all I could think about was the fact that society expects this guy to manage his own pension plan. Not to mention he's got a free license to reproduce. Where's the director? Maybe she should have done his vasectomy profile while he was here and see if he qualified."

"Do you think the government should be more involved in retirement? I thought you were the big libertarian," said Alvarez.

"The government would do it worse," said Maglio. "I don't have an answer. But it confirms my plan to retire to some banana republic and keep all my money off shore."

"What will you do when the banana republic overthrows the intellectuals and you get kicked out?" asked Alvarez.

"They're not too bright if they think I'm intellectual. I looked up the records on the same guy though, the pill guy. He comes in one day for anxiety and that he can't sleep. He gets a prescription for a sleeping pill, goes home, takes it, calls an ambulance an hour later because he's too sleepy. What do you say to that guy? I can't cure stupid."

Jerry had crouched down by the radiology computer terminal and was unplugging and rearranging wires. He stood up smiling. "I couldn't do a deep knee bend like that before I died. Well, not for about ten years anyway."

"Jerry, I need to step outside."

"Suit yourself."

"Do you think I'll be all right if I go too far from here?"

"What are you scared of, the neighborhood?"

"Actually yes. But not today, being as I am dead. I mean, if I go too far away from me, me in the intensive care unit, do you think I might not be able to get back?"

"Look Cheese. I have no idea. I'm not the expert on these sorts of experiences. But I think if you can find your way across Michigan Avenue and back, you can probably get right back into the ER and I'll be here waiting."

"Do you think there are more of us, you know, walking around out there?"

"Ghosts?"

"Exactly."

"How the hell would I know? You know, I used to ask this one guy a lot of advice. He was over a hundred. I think he was a hundred and six when he died. He came through the dialysis unit because he used to get blood transfusions once in a while. Name was Clarence. He had some kind of blood cancer that's slow to progress and his docs had figured out he was going to die of something else before the cancer got him so they just transfused him some blood once in a while if he needed it. Pretty rational approach, right?

I had just lost Millie and I was having my own health problems and Clarence seemed to have it together. He moved around pretty good on his feet and everything. So I asked him what his secret to longevity and health was. He told me it was cigars in the evening and jalapeno peppers in the morning. I told him I didn't believe him. You know what the old geezer said? First I thought he'd keel over because when Clarence laughed he would start wheezing and get kind of blue but it was usually temporary. This time he laughed so hard I wasn't sure. But when he finally came around he said, 'I have gotten asked that question so many times since I turned a hundred that I got sick of it. I think I lived this long by dumb luck mostly. But nobody wants to hear that. And I figure if they take the trouble to ask, I should give them a good answer. I started making up stuff this past year and boy, has it been fun. The tribune even interviewed me for some health feature and I told the reporter that my secret was barbecued lemons and Jack Daniels and they printed it. I told a radio show that is was pickled eggs and sky diving. People make such a big deal out of the number. You even get a little auto-signed birthday card from the president. Mine came three years late.'

Clarence was a helluva guy. I wouldn't mind running into him on the other side. After that I asked him less advice. But I started to mess with folks a little more. Don't take it personally, Alan. And if you want to people watch, there's a great sandwich shop under the L track called Solly's. They have great hotdogs and they make a falafel burger to die for," Jerry cackled at his own joke.

I was going to tell him he didn't look like the falafel burger type but just then the doors whisked open for another paramedic crew and a gust of brisk air followed them in. I glanced at the young woman on the stretcher who was chatting on her cell phone and then I went outside. I didn't want to meet anyone else dead or half-dead. Jerry wasn't that bad. There were probably some much angrier dead people. I might run into a dead terrorist whose seventeen virgins weren't what they had been billed. Talk about a double vendetta then. And how many people died with all their affairs in order any way? Family clustered around a bed with eiderdown covers and the nearly deceased propped up on goose down pillows giving personalized advice to every family member. If I had to do that then I definitely wasn't ready to go. I wouldn't have a clue what to say in advice.

The parking lot was busier than I expected. A lot of smokers were clustered slightly out of the wind under the big red sign that announced that St. Augustine's was an entirely smoke-free campus. Other people milled around in the parking lot, either stretching their legs while their loved ones received medical treatment or perhaps just looking for a car to break into. It was hard to tell the difference. I scanned the cars and didn't see Laura's. Jerry might have been right, at least about Kevin driving her home. The incessant beeping and blinking alarms of the ER monitors were replaced by the sound of traffic, sirens, and the rumble of the L train overhead. I stared up and felt like I was witnessing a miracle. The train was a thing of beauty. Here I was dead, and I could still watch the L train make its curve and head west to the next station.

I hardly ever drove to the office. The train was quicker and even if I missed the express I could doze in the warm air or watch the skyline on the way in to the city.

The clackety and screech of brakes slowed and stopped with a hiss. I could just see the surge of people through the grating above me, bundled in coats and carrying bags, coming and going, climbing the iron stairs to the next platform over to catch the line that ran north. Instinctively, I made my way toward the station. There was Solly's. It looked like a dive, not really the sort of place I would usually go to. I had been to St. Augustine's a handful of times, contrary to what Jerry might think of my suburban status. My aunt lived in the neighborhood and spent a week in the hospital for pneumonia.

The windows of Solly's were steamed into a haze and all I could make out was that it was crowded. The front door opened in clouds of steam as patrons made their exit with take-out bags. Some of them wore scrubs under their coats and must have come from the hospital. I went in and found an empty place to stand near the pick-up window. The decorations were still hanging: a Santa with limbs akimbo thumb-tacked next to the grease board menu, a tinseled artificial tree by the cash register, and a garish baby New Year poster above the kitchen swinging doors.

"Gyro platter, gyro platter, falafel side, falafel burger, gyro sandwich, all go," shouted the man taking orders to the direction of the kitchen. A paper ticket went up and spun around. The lamb roasts turned on their spits and the man in the kitchen sliced off fresh pieces.

"Next."

"I'll take a number two and a medium drink."

"Gyro platter , falafel side, all go, here's your cup, pick up over there, next!"

The place was busy and being right under the L they had extra traffic no matter the time of day. For a moment my anxiety about being dead ebbed. I could just sit down with a lunch, get back to my office before close of business and catch the train back out to the burbs in time for prime time TV.

The train roared to life over our heads and for a moment even the bark of the order taker was silenced by the rumble. It faded away and the volume in Solly's resumed.

A group of hippy dressed college kids picked up bags of falafel to go. I still couldn't picture Jerry biding his time here, waiting for dialysis.

The front doors opened again and the steam billowed out. In its place was Raymond. He carried a St. Augustine's belongings bag, the sort of drawstring bag they throw your worldly goods in when you check in or check out. He had two other plastic bags slung over his shoulder and the misshapen coat wrapped around his thin frame. He looked directly at me and squinted. He rubbed his eyes and stared harder. I was standing right by the wall; there couldn't have been anyone behind me. I looked over my shoulder at the wall. Nothing written on it. I looked back at Raymond. Could he really see me? He didn't look like a ghost, but, I supposed, neither did I.

"Traveler," he said. He was still looking right at me. His face was lined beyond his age and he had a zigzag of scars along one side and down his neck. His nose actually did go in three different directions from the bridge to the tip, just like True had said.

"Hey, I told you last time not to keep coming back in here. You need me to call the cops?" It was the man behind the counter who had noticed the vagrant.

Raymond turned his attention away from me.

"Christians?"

The man behind the counter groaned. "Raymond, I'm not going to go into this today. You need to move it along."

"Man, I'm hungry. You call yourselves Christian?"

"We call ourselves a restaurant. Come on Raymond, we got customers."

"God made the grape."

"Right. And in your case, he made the potato, the barley, the hops, and the crack pipe. Move it along."

He looked toward me again and squinted at the wall. "Traveler," he said again.

"Are you talking to me?" I asked.

He didn't say anything. He turned and opened the front door and left.

I decided to follow.

He was headed down the street under the L, still talking to himself. Although it probably didn't matter, I kept a safe distance. The mass of commuters and shoppers on the sidewalk carried us along until he turned down an alley. I swallowed my doubts and followed him. The snow was grey and grimy and would remain that way until it melted. The melting snow dripped through the train platform grates above my head. It was getting late in the afternoon but in the alley, unlit and narrow between two tall buildings, it may as well have been night.

"Traveler, find rest. They will never know what you see. They don't know nothing. They just don't know nothing," said Raymond.

He couldn't have been talking to me, I was too far behind him. I scanned the boxes and debris on either side of me as I made my way down the alley, afraid of who might be there. I had to admit, I wished Jerry was along. He wouldn't have been nervous in the alley. He would have been pulling pranks on the vagrants.

But I think I was alone. Other than Raymond, that is. He was back on the street in the next block, just a short cut, and to my surprise he headed into the L station. He moved quickly when he wanted to. I walked quickly to keep up before he was out of sight and just caught a glimpse of him climbing over a turnstile. There was nobody in the ticket booth at this station. Raymond must have known.

I reached for my pockets and then, shrugging, climbed over the turnstile myself. Now that was something I had never done before. It hadn't been on the bucket list but I mentally added it and then checked it. If there was one thing I knew in the city, it was how to get around on the train and the tracks made a neat box around the city and would circle back to the stop next to St. Augustine's.

Raymond was ten paces ahead of me on the stairs. The other commuters gave him a wide berth and he got onto the north bound blue line car. He sat down in the handicapped seat and spread out his bags. Taking out a bottle from one of his pockets, he continued his conversation.

"Rest for the weary they say. Rest for the meek. Ain't nothing for the meek. The mission would make me their servant. I serve the traveler. Unless you can stay a step ahead they will pull you in," he took a long sip and gestured at the businesswoman several rows back. "That's why I retired so early. Never let them make you one of them, them that's made it just made it on your back, you know the truth." He shouted the last word and the woman opened her purse and carefully inspected its contents. I leaned my head over and saw that she had a canister of pepper spray on her keychain. I hoped I wasn't susceptible to that any more. My wife had the same sort of thing in her purse and she sprayed it once in the house on the day she bought it, just to make sure it worked. My eyes watered, I coughed so hard I nearly threw up, and I couldn't get the smell out of my suit coat until I took it to the cleaners. I would have been a very ineffective rioter.

My children might have inherited Laura's tolerance to the stuff. She said it made her sneeze a little bit, nothing more, and couldn't understand how it was going to be any use against an assailant. But the two kids at college might need it if they marched against the war. Did they still tear gas college kids, I wondered? It seemed contrary to the kinder gentler age we lived in. Then again, the protesters usually stayed on campus and it was more of a walk in the park carrying signs for the upper body work out than anything else. If I could talk to them again, I would tell them both to find a cause. They needed something to fight for. They could forgo all the trappings of comfort when they were young enough to not need it. Except maybe a condo. They might want a condo, low payments, just something to fall back on when the cause was achieved. Or in case they were on the lam.

That would have been a much better way to go out. On the lam and down in flames. Give the kids something to talk about after they flew back to school. Hopefully they had the sense to get a roundtrip emergency plane ticket. Cheaper in the long run. But being on the lam might have voided my life insurance policy. I was pretty sure there was a clause in there about criminal activity.

The train eased to a stop with the usual unintelligible announcements. Raymond settled into the seat and his bottle. I knew that around the next turn was the view of the skyline that I looked forward to on every ride.

I wished I had a falafel burger. I didn't know if I could eat or not but I would have just held the bag, felt the warmth, inhaled the spicy scent. A briefcase would have been good too. I would have felt more put together. I was pretty sure Laura was going to give me a new briefcase for my birthday this year. She had been hinting about dimensions and shades of cowhide and that she couldn't find something before the holidays. I could get one that had compartments for all the new electronic gadgets. An electronic reader, a phone that could access the internet, a separate pouch for all the chargers, maybe a solar powered strip for a conversation starter. I could carry a battered old paperback novel with me too, just for the irony. Something antiestablishment. Maybe the Vonnegut I used to read in college. Yes, I would tell people, the solar charger really comes in handy when I am off the grid. Where do I go off the grid? Oh nothing I could really discuss. But I save the Vonnegut for cloudy days. Which suits the literature. At which point I would laugh knowingly and see if anyone laughed with me.

I would carry my new briefcase through the turnstile, find my seat and pull out a baguette. My new routine would include a sophisticated breakfast on the train. Brie. I would even put brie on the baguette. Except I would have to find out whether to eat that outer part that felt like wax. It didn't spread at all well and I never knew if it was edible. So I never bought brie. What a way to live. Having dealt with Jerry for a mere hour or two, I was definitely ready to handle any sneers from the posh section of the dairy counter. I would simply walk up to the counter the next time and ask whether that part of the brie was edible. Maybe I could use an accent. I could tell them I was from somewhere that didn't have cheese. But that would take some research to pick a place. Maybe I could ask if it was the brie with the edible crust or the other kind of brie. Then, if they told me that of course it was edible or of course it wasn't, I would still have the upper hand in making them think there was another kind of brie that they didn't know about. God, I hated the cheese counter. Laura had sent me there when we were having some friends over and she was making some potato cheese thing that was in pie crust and the timing of everything had to be just so. She had said the name of the cheese so fast that at the time I pretended to know what she was talking about. But the cheese counter guy gave me that look, the same look he'd given me when I mispronounced Neufchatel, and told me that there was no such thing. So I confidently told him "Of course there is, I told you I needed a pound of dill havarti," which was the first thing I saw inside the glass case. He rolled his eyes, packaged up the order, and Laura never sent me to the cheese counter again.

I could even strike up a conversation with one of the college girls. None my daughter's age. One of the graduate students. Nothing beyond a few witty remarks. I dabbled in accounting, yes. My main passion was anti-matter. Why yes, I had done a little research for NASA. Nothing I could really talk about, you know. Very hush-hush. This novel? Just an old Vonnegut. I dusted it off when I came back from Madagascar. When I was off the grid. Shoot, I shouldn't have mentioned that. And they would tell their friends about the fascinating yet understated man they had met on the train who had a solar charger for his gear.

I missed my briefcase. I don't think Laura knew, but I often borrowed her alumnae magazine when it came and brought it along to read on the train. I would tuck it under my laptop in the morning and slide it into the laptop compartment. None of the schools I had gone to published anything of the sort. She had gone to a tony prep school that ran K through twelve and engendered more loyalty than most nations. Especially among the "lifers" as they liked to be called.

With as much grief as I gave her about the cost of our granddaughter's education, I would never have admitted to her how much I liked reading the class notes section. The fact that Harold "Harry" '41 was still playing golf twice a week despite his hip replacement, or that Whitney '99 had married Clive '97 in a lovely outdoor ceremony in Saratoga, or that Blake '62 had a grandson studying abroad on a Fulbright somehow filled me with ease as the train rattled through downtown. It was always done with such a positive spin. By the time the alum had penned the letter to their class correspondent, he or she had had enough time to find the right words to announce the divorce or corporate downsizing as a great opportunity to live the studio apartment lifestyle again and spend more time with the book club. I had no idea who any of these people were. But they sounded wonderful. The next time I was in Saratoga I was sure I could stop in on Whitney and Clive and impart some generational advice, alum-in-law to alum and ask if they too had heard the news about Harry's golf game.

Another thought struck me however. Laura would announce my death in the class notes. In fact the submission deadline was in two weeks. I knew this because with the holidays just behind us she had been griping about not having time to send in her submission. I had told her to just cut and paste something from the family letter that she wrote with the Christmas cards but she insisted that it needed a different tone.

Would she have enough time to get the wording right?

'Laura Fries '79 sent the sad news that her husband Alan passed away suddenly but peacefully after a brave but brief battle with ventricular tachycardia and a defibrillator in their friends' living room. Fortunately he participated in an important clinical trial on the role of induced hypothermia in sudden cardiac arrest that mainly involved ice packs in uncomfortable places and was thus able to make a great contribution to the field of medicine after a long and rewarding career as an accountant. In happier news, Laura is attending evening yoga twice a week with classmates Courtney '79 and Whitney '79 and both ladies can now do the full sun salutation without any hand held notes.'

I wondered if someone was assigned to write obituaries at the newspapers or if the family had to provide the script. When my parents had died, my brother had been the executor and he had handled whatever part that had required.

There was Graham and Graham's building. The smokers were banished outside and had congregated under the eaves of the side door in communion. The administrative staff was starting to leave. Not the accountants. I had nearly finished the McMillan case and had been meaning to call him. The attempt to claim his pool as a health deduction hadn't worked last year and he was trying it again but calling it a non-surgical weight reduction strategy this time. And he was claiming his boomerang son who was unemployed and living at home as an employee. The last missive from McMillan contained instructions to deduct his son's "salary" as pool cleaner at over a hundred thousand for the year as a business expense and I had not crafted a reply yet as to why I could do no such thing. He also had some documents that showed his son paying someone else eighty thousand a year to be his personal assistant. I think

McMillan's theory was to keep paying assistants like those Russian nesting dolls until his actual tax liability was twenty seven cents. It's not that I would get into trouble if he was audited. We had enough contract language to protect the accountant from their client's misdeeds. But there was an unspoken directive to save clients from their own stupidity. And the thought of having to go through all of McMillan's receipts if he was audited was enough to make me consider staying dead. Or at least in a coma through the end of April. Actually the McMillan case was only slightly better than death. I would need to think that one over. When I started my own firm, I would take the good clients but Graham and Graham could keep McMillan.

Sleep would be good. What was the point of death or near-death if I couldn't even fall asleep? Maybe when I was discharged from the hospital I could get them to prescribe some sort of sleeping pill. Not that I would use it all the time but it might come in handy if I had to meet with McMillan. I could put one in his sparkling water, take his box of receipts and run. Usually the motion of the train and the class notes would have done the trick by now. Even Raymond was snoring. I looked up at the window nearest me. There was a spider web stretched from the corner of the window to the ceiling and a small black spider was sitting on the window ledge, walking a few inches forward, then darting back, seemingly unsure of how to proceed. A winter spider, I thought. What on earth did it find to eat this time of year in the train?

Laura and I had received the obligatory corporate Christmas card from Graham and Graham. The past few years, each Graham had been sending out their own card as a family photo rather than the stuffier business version. The first year they did that I thought it was sort of identity theft scam. Here was this card with a tanned, smiling, silver haired guy in mirrored sunglasses with his arm around a blonde, tanned, smiling woman in a tank top. All it was said was "Happy Holidays from Louis and Arlene. We're enjoying our usual trip to South Beach." I had no idea who they were. I certainly didn't know anyone who took a "usual" trip to South Beach. The feigned familiarity made me suspicious that the next card would be a request for Western Union money from old friend

Louis. That sort of thing was running rampant. I was just about to turn the return address in to the police when Laura remembered that she thought the Grahams were Louis Sr. and Louis Jr.

What clinched it was the next card. It was a picture of a younger man than the first Louis with a similar nose. He sat demurely next to a demure wife and spread around them were four very well-groomed children in matching winter white sweaters. The family was dressed up for the photo except they all were barefoot. It was clearly a deliberate move. It just couldn't have been at the last minute they all forgot footwear. To this day I don't know if it was a John Lennon tribute or some bizarre way to seem down to earth or just casual. It was signed "Louis and Ashley." I was pretty sure that if I turned up on Louis and Ashley's door step, barefoot or not, I would not be let in. One of these days I will get good and loaded at the office holiday party and corner Louis Jr. and demand an explanation. And after that I will admonish him to never do it again. He had those uncomfortably long toes and while his wife's feet weren't too bad, the children had definitely inherited the toe gene from their father. The sight of so many toes on a Christmas card was unnerving.

It was snowing. The visibility through the windows closed to a few yards as the snow gusted and swirled. That was too bad because the train was rounding the stretch of track where I could get a glimpse of Lake Michigan on a clear day. In the winter there was a shelf of ice that stretched about a hundred yards out from shore. I had never walked out on it although I had driven my car into one of the parks and watched the distant waves through the windshield. Every winter more than one person walked too far out on the shelf and drowned. Or froze. I suppose it was both. I wondered if that led to more paperwork glitches if the coroner couldn't decide on the exact cause of death. I didn't understand the impulse to go out there. It was beyond freezing. Even on a calm day in winter it felt like a gale force wind that close to the lake.

I sometimes watched that show about crab fishermen in Alaska. It was usually on late and if I couldn't sleep I would go downstairs and flip through the channels. I was fascinated by the freezing cold brutality of their existence. Everything on the boat looked painful from the ice encrusted chains that hauled up the traps, to the frozen metal tools used to open and shut them, to the writhing crabs themselves with claws waving. One man on the show lost a finger to frostbite but he kept the shriveled digit and had it made into a necklace. I couldn't get over that. The sheer guts.

I didn't have any stories like that exactly. Nothing I could throw down at the bar and get people to buy me rounds of drinks. A peg leg. A scar. A finger made into a necklace.

There was the raccoon that we trapped in the attic. Well, I hired a guy who came and trapped the raccoon. But it was in our attic. Our granddaughter was over for the morning and it all started when the dog kept digging up the yard. It was getting bad, just pot holes everywhere. One of the neighbors told Laura that there might be mice in the flower beds or voles and since the dog was a terrier it would be irresistible. Get rid of the rodents and the dog would stop digging. So we called a guy who came out and surveyed the yard. He put a few decorative traps that had rodent poison in them, big plastic domes that were supposed to look like rocks. He walked around the yard a few times and asked if we had any raccoons still in the attic.

That seemed like a loaded question to me. The sort of thing my older brother used to ask me when I was a kid that drove me nuts, like, when did you stop stealing?

Still in the attic? Had we ever had raccoons in the attic?

He pointed out the bent louvers on an attic vent, climbed up a ladder and walked around and shouted down that he saw fresh raccoon dropping on the roof. By now our granddaughter was outside and enjoying the fact that some guy was walking around on the roof. He came down from the ladder and asked if she would like to see a real raccoon. He just happened to have one in his truck from another job he had come from.

Next thing we knew, the animal control guy was toting around a box trap with a hissing, cowering raccoon in it and Clare was delighted.

Come to think of it we had heard some rustling noises at night but I had always thought it was just the house settling. Or wind.

He left the house having placed a box trap at an odd angle on the roof. It looked like something one would use to trap leprechauns. Climbing down from the ladder, Clare watched through the living room window and announced excitedly "He's done putting the raccoon in the attic."

I had patted her on the head and told her that he had left the trap up there and took the other raccoon to a nice place far away in the woods with other raccoons but I had always wondered about that. Generating business. Take whatever was trapped at one place and move it to your next customer. It would provide job security. It wasn't that different from the world of finance.

I wondered if anyone went on Lake Michigan in the winter. It was strange I had never thought of it before. The train windows rattled from an easterly gust as if to answer that. Laura and I could learn to sail in the summer. That had to be a fairly easy paced exercise. Not having to contend with ice covered crab pots would be a start. Except I was frightened of water. Not in a paralyzing sense. No, I knew how to swim and paddle a canoe. Summer camp had made sure of it. But one summer when I had first gone out in the canoe, it was a little lake in Wisconsin, just about five miles long, I began to doubt my sense of direction. We were in a group of eight canoes. I was in the middle of the caravan and each canoe had two paddlers. My partner was a kid named Grant. He came from a family where everyone sounded like they owned their own complement of outdoor equipment for any eventuality, right down to snow shoes and snorkeling gear. I tended to borrow mine. Not because my family couldn't afford it but because they didn't know what half of it was for and consequently didn't know that I needed it.

We had been paddling for about thirty minutes when I was hit by a panic. I hadn't made any sort of mental note as to what our dock looked like and as I glanced over my shoulder, I was dismayed to see that they all looked alike.

I mentioned this to Grant and he scoffed at me.

"It's that one," he said.

"Which one? They all look alike," I said.

He pointed vaguely with his paddle. "The one over there. Besides, the instructor knows where it is. It's not like we're out here alone."

Grant struck me as someone who had never been let down. The instructor was three canoes ahead of us and was paddling without a care. He was the same guy that made it through a half hearted version of 'Let it Be' on the guitar in the bunk room and then left with the other camp counselors most evenings to go smoke by the lake, leaving the campers to our own devices in the cabins. They had it made, because by the time night fell, we were all scared enough of the woods that nobody would have tried to leave the cabin. Supervision ended with sunset and paranoia took over. In retrospect, maybe that was the point of ghost stories after dinner. It guaranteed curfew compliance. So to say the least, I wasn't convinced the instructor knew where he was leading us. The least they could do was tie some balloons on the pier. Or streamers. I didn't think Grant knew which one it was. Of course, if everyone tied balloons or streamers on their pier they would start to all look alike that way too.

I told Grant that we were lost.

He sighed. "The lake is a big circle Alan. We'll come back to the pier eventually."

"Only if we go around the whole thing. Do you know how far that is? It's a circumference. It would take us three days. If we cut across the middle we might hit the wrong halfway point."

We eventually made it back to the pier. But I remember feeling unsettled for the rest of that trip. For the rest of the summer camp I signed up for technique classes where I could practice different ways to paddle and stay within a short lap of the pier.

My sense of direction improved after that. Laura and I had taken a dinner cruise last summer in fact. Granted we stayed in sight of the shore but I knew that the shoreline was west and therefore the rest was easy. I think she had even been impressed by my lingo about the winds being southeasterly over the port side as we headed south. The waiter had rolled his eyes when he heard me say it but I'm pretty sure I had it right. I don't think Laura noticed and I picked out a bottle of red from the mid price range to keep the waiter happy.

The train lurched to a stop and the doors opened. Two kids got on, maybe high school age, in hooded sweatshirts. They were loud and it woke up Raymond.

"Man, look at that guy."

"What a waste, man."

"You got any cigarettes in that coat?" the first kid asked. They stood on either side of Raymond's seat and leaned over him.

"Got no smokes," Raymond answered. "I got the answer, though. You on the wrong train."

The kids laughed. "That's pretty good. You think we're on the wrong train, huh? You want to tell us which train to ride? You better apologize."

Raymond kicked the first kid just under the knee cap. He fell hard and landed on the train floor. Raymond reached up and grabbed the second kid by the front of his sweatshirt and pulled him forward. He landed, face-first, against the side of the train. The first kid rolled on the floor holding his leg. The second kid clutched his bloody nose.

The next thing I realized, the businesswoman from the other row was on her feet, standing over the kid on the floor. She efficiently pepper sprayed him and then sprayed his friend. She aimed it toward Raymond, then must have decided against it and instead sat back down. The train lurched to its next stop. Raymond was unfazed by the pepper spray ambiance at first. Then he coughed, coughed again, and vomited onto the kid's feet with the bloody nose. One more cough and Raymond settled back into his seat. He adjusted his coat back around himself and watched the two kids hobble through the sliding doors to the platform. "I told you that you were on the wrong train," he called after them as the doors closed and we lurched forward again.

It was then that I realized I had been holding my breath. I took a shaky breath in and was relieved that the pepper spray didn't affect me in my present condition. At least something was going right today. The whole thing had happened so quickly. Raymond was back to dozing in his seat. I wondered how often he had to do that sort of thing. The businesswoman looked around angrily and the other passengers mostly avoided looking her way, afraid that she still had pepper spray to spray. All the time I had ridden the train, the most criminal activity I had seen before was a purse snatching. Kids today. I wonder if someone made a hypoallergenic pepper spray. It wouldn't do me any good to carry it otherwise.

Chapter 5

Jerry convinced me that the department committee meeting of the hospital should be our next stop. I didn't share his enthusiasm but he emphasized we could always throw paperclips if things got too slow and at that point, I didn't have any better ideas. The interlude on the train, which I had hoped would give me perspective, only left me feeling worse because when it was over, I was back at St. Augustine's.

We stood in the hallway for a moment. Out of the corner of my eye, I spotted another hand washing station. "We share our mission, not our germs," the sign said. They really did have them everywhere. I couldn't resist: I waved my hands under the paper towel dispenser. Nothing.

"Will you stop doing that!" Jerry said.

"I'm just checking," I replied.

"Checking if you're still dead? The fact that we just walked down a hallway and nobody noticed anything didn't clue you in?"

"We look like normal people. If someone saw us walk by they wouldn't necessarily say anything."

Jerry swung his fist at my stomach and I watched it pass through.

"Don't do that!" I said.

"Believe me?"

"Yes, but that just feels creepy. Look I have a theory."

Jerry rolled his eyes.

"Since they're trying to bring me back upstairs, you know, in the ICU, I thought I might slowly come back down here. Like maybe I might start to have more weight. I saw a science fiction movie where they did that."

"Enough gravitas to set off the paper towel motion detector? That's quite a goal, Cheese."

"It's just an example. And since they have them every ten feet apparently, it happens to be a convenient one. Besides, I don't understand why I can pick up stuff but I can't set off a motion detector."

Jerry waved his hands under it. Nothing.

"It's making you act like an obsessive-compulsive nut. Besides, I think you have it backwards. If you get resuscitated upstairs then you will have less presence down here. And the difference is the motion detector part. We're invisible, in case you didn't notice. No visible motion."

"You think so?" I asked. "I thought they worked on infra-red."

"Christ, I don't know," said Jerry. "The bigger problem is I don't know if I would trust a doctor that has to be reminded to wash his hands by a slogan. I think we're turning into a society of robots. Buy a pill online. Cures all ills. Vote for me," he grumbled.

He had a point. I watched enviously as a passing doctor in the hallway went to the same station and turned on the water. He was humming "Happy Birthday."

"Jerry, did you write your own obituary or did someone else do it?"

"I don't know."

"What do you mean you don't know?"

"I mean I didn't write it and I don't know if someone else did. Don't care. Can't think of many people around who would want to read it and those you would want to read it could write it themselves."

"But wouldn't you want to plan what it said? What if they got something wrong?"

"Only point of an obituary is to give the living something to cut out of the newspaper and stick in a book somewhere. I could care less what it said. Actually, I could care less what it said as long as it didn't go into what a blessing it was that I was called home and all that nonsense. Have you ever met these death fetishists? I swear they think they will score points with God by spending time with the dying and bragging to their friends about how beautiful it all is. It's not. One of my cousins got religion about two months before she died of cancer and she fell in with the crew that thinks they have God on speed dial. I wasn't going to say anything to her, it gave her comfort in her last days you know. But one of those do-gooders had the nerve to stand up at the funeral and give a speech about how he had only known her for two days but in those two days she had changed his life because of her inspirational love of God. What a bunch of malarkey. What kind of a creep goes and hangs around somebody dying in a matter of days and then thinks they can give a speech at the funeral. Like he knew her at all. I would have decked him but my other cousin took care of it later in the parking lot."

"He beat him up in the parking lot?"

"He decked him. There's a difference, Alan. Decking is corrective."

"But still. A fight broke out at a family funeral. Did that happen a lot in your family?"

"Exactly Alan. A family funeral. This self righteous pole smoker had no business being there. I think they were after her money anyways. You know, get her to leave it to their church. Haven't you ever had to deck someone?" he looked at me and I think he answered his own question.

"Never mind. But chasing them off my porch was sometimes fun. The same evangelical nutwads used to ring my doorbell and try to give me literature on who knows what. I thought that if I told them I was dying it would make them go away but instead they wanted to go on and on about what a blessing it was to be called home. I told them death would have been a blessing compared to listening to them. That didn't make them leave so I told them death would have been a blessing about three years ago before I had to go on methadone from the cancer and I could only crap once a week. After that death wasn't so much of a blessing as it was about damn time." "You were on methadone?"

"Everybody's on it. Come on. I had tumors in the bone. You better believe I was on methadone. Who are you to talk? You're the one who came back after narcan."

"Oh please, I thought we resolved that. Do you really still think I'm a heroin user?"

"Not any more. When I first met you, maybe."

I wasn't sure if I should thank him. Part of me was annoyed that he so readily dismissed the possibility of my using something illicit.

"How did you finally chase them off your porch?"

"I invited them in to watch some porn and share my Jack Daniels."

"Nobody took you up on it?"

"They never traveled alone. Somebody would have ratted the other guy out."

I let the issue rest and followed Jerry. I had gone to my share of meetings and never would have guessed I would attend one posthumously. But maybe it would take my mind off maybe being dead. The staff was all gathered in a room just off the library. There was a formica table and a hodgepodge of chairs. The nurse manager, a stocky woman of about fifty, opened the meeting by reviewing the statistics of the month.

The director had a folder with her.

"I have a comment from a patient that I will share. Is Gabrielle the satisfaction expert here yet?"

Jerry elbowed me. "I told you this meeting might be good."

"She's not coming today. With the upcoming change in administration we decided to keep the ancillary departments out of the meetings until the corporate change. No offense," said the manager.

"Until the hostile takeover. None taken. Very well. Take this as my two cents and you can do with it what you like since I have to spend an hour of my day here in the first place."

I was trying to gauge the response of the minions at the meeting. Clearly some were on the director's side but didn't want to admit it.

Jerry was whispering again. "That nurse manager is the quintessential bureaucrat. Guaranteed to have a long, stable, pointless, and mediocre career. She hasn't laid hands on another human being in over ten years and that probably includes her husband..."

The director continued. "Many other busy ERs have our problems. Too many patients for the number of rooms that we have. Challenges in patient flow. There are ways we could make better use of the footprint that we have."

"I like her," Jerry whispered.

"You don't have to whisper," I reminded him.

"She's smart. And she has great legs," he said, "and she could always find an IV in my neck on the first try when nobody else could. One shot, one kill kind of doc. She's probably great in the sack."

"Shh!" I hissed.

"But we don't have to whisper," Jerry said.

"A patient who spent a total of six hours in our ER wrote a letter of complaint that is actually full of great ideas. She says 'I have been coming to your hospital for a long time. I expect it to be busy and I expect to have to wait. However, I have needed blood transfusions twice in the past and when I came in last week I felt the same way. I waited in your waiting room for over two hours before I even got into a room. Why couldn't you draw my blood and at least run the test that I came for while I was waiting? If it came back normal then I wouldn't even need to be in your ER and you could use the bed for someone who was really sick?' I called her after getting this letter and told her this type of thing was being done in other hospitals as far as starting the work up from the waiting room."

"It would never work here," said the manager.

"Why not?" asked the director. I had a sense she had had this conversation before.

"Because our patient population is different. They wouldn't understand it if we were running tests and not putting them in a room. It's never been done that way here. You can't let the patient dictate what we test. Can you believe her nerve? The test I came for. Next thing you know people will want MRI scans from the waiting room because they read about something on the internet and now they're convinced they have some horrible disease."

The director was several shades of red brighter than she had been a moment before. Jerry was watching with glee, I think hoping for a cat fight. I was actually interested in the debate. I had never heard this sort of 'us versus them' mentality from the realm of healthcare before but from the director's battle-weary tone I had a sense it might be all too common-place.

"Our patients wouldn't understand? Why? Are you really saying poor people are stupid?"

"Don't be ridiculous."

"Don't be so judgmental then. I have never had a problem with an informed patient. And I don't see a difference between the burbs or the hood when it comes to medical understanding. Maybe they brought some misinformation from the internet with them or they were overworried about their kid. Big deal. That's what we're here for. To teach. To allay fears. Every once in a while we get to do something cool like you see on TV. But you know most of the time we're just reassuring people that the sniffles is not the latest imported bird flu. And you're saying our patients wouldn't understand the concept of 'wait here for your test results?' That is absurd," the director said. She turned to the nursing student assigned to take minutes. "Will you please note that the nursing director thinks our patients are too stupid to understand how to wait for a test result."

"Don't you dare put that in there," barked the manager.

"Then give me a better reason why you think we can't do this."

The nursing student looked between the two of them with eyes like saucers, hands poised over the laptop computer.

"There are regulations, you know," the manager continued, sounding more confident. "There are airflow regulation as far as how many cubic feet an exam room needs to be."

"Is that the real reason?" asked the director.

"It's a regulation," the manager replied, stretching out the syllables and glaring.

"Or what happens?" asked the director.

"What do you mean? Nothing happens. Except if the commission inspects your facility and you aren't regulation you will fail and get fined. A lot. Other than that nothing else happens."

"And they enforce these airflow cubic feet regulations a lot do they?"

"Of course," the manager answered smugly, smelling acquiescence.

"The how many cubic feet of air do we need per patient in the waiting room?"

I smiled at the reaction. Trapped. It was too bad that from what I had gathered the director was going to a different hospital.

"I'm not sure but I fail to see the relevance."

"Two hundred cubic feet. And right now given that we have forty-seven patients in the waiting room, we would need to kick forty of them outside into the parking lot to provide enough airflow to circulate the flu virus around or whatever these ridiculous guidelines are aiming for so my point is that at the moment, precisely now, you are in violation of the airflow policy you seek to enforce. Do you want me to go tell security to enact our disaster plan and set up the big tent in the parking lot since we are so overwhelmed?"

"The inspectors don't go to the waiting room and beside other hospitals in the city have this problem too."

"Yes they do. Which is why St. Pat's hired me." The director paused and looked down the line of nursing supervisors gathered around the table. "And I think they are hiring nurses the last time I checked. Their nurse manager even works a few shifts in the ER from what I have been told. Yes, she touches patients. What a radical concept. It's a progressive place. I would be happy to put in a good word."

Glares. I was amazed. Jerry was practically drooling. Was this what it was like when one had nothing to lose? Frankly it wasn't fair. I could tell off the man if I knew I was going to stay dead. Except no one could see me or hear me. Of all the rotten irony. It was better than telling off the man. It was telling off the man and telling him how to do it better. Except this was telling off the woman.

"By the way, how have the nursing ratios been lately?" the director asked.

"I don't know what you mean; they've been fine," the manager said.

"Really? They were nine to one yesterday. Do you think that's safe?"

"We had hours on the schedule that nobody picked up. We're fully staffed. We just have to encourage the staff to pick up hours when they need to be filled."

"They cut your staff twenty percent in the last cycle didn't they?" asked the director.

"Not in every department," the manager countered.

"Look, you don't need to defend the administration to me. Not behind closed doors at least. I just want the other nurses to know that this is the same shell game that plays out before a hospital closes. Cut personnel but leave the hours there so everything looks good on paper. Blame the remaining staff for not wanting to work eighty or more hours a week and voila, three holes in the schedule and nine to one staffing ratios but of course it wasn't intentional," said the director, drawing a circle with hash marks through it on her notepad for emphasis. "It saves a lot of hourly money though, doesn't it? Maybe it's something we should discuss when the joint commission is here this week?"

"I do not need you discussing any nursing issues when the joint commission is here. Just make sure Dr. Maglio isn't eating pizza at the work station when they walk through and we'll be fine," the manager snapped.

The director scribbled on her notepad and then read it. "Joint commission. Dr. Maglio to bring pizza for department." She looked up brightly. "Got it."

More glares. I didn't see the nurse with the tattoos. She must not have been in the inner circle.

I wanted Laura to go back to work. I could recuperate. Do some light activity around the house, run the leaf blower in the fall, supervise the guys cleaning the gutters to make sure they did what they billed for. Laura could go back to work and come home with tales of corporate escapades. She had great ankles. Great legs in general but beautiful ankles for her age. I told her that once but I had included the 'for your age' part and it hadn't gone over well. But she could go back to work and wear heels again. Hostile takeovers. Malfiescience. Except Laura might be very good at it. God, what if she met someone else in the process? She would be telling her sad tale about her invalid husband, she'd talk about it wearing heels and a suit with her feet up on her desk and some vice president would take pity on her and the next thing anybody knew they would have a torrid affair.

No. It would be better if I came back to life robust and devil may care. I could stride into the next Graham and Graham staff meeting, one of the rare ones that Mr. Graham actually attended, and tell them exactly what I thought. The older Mr. Graham, that is, not the guy's son. Come to think of it I had never really met the guy's son. Maybe the rumors that he spent his time in Abu Dhabi on his father's dole were correct. But I would tell his father what for. I would lay it all out there that the pension plan was half-baked and the benefits for pre-tax vision check-ups didn't go nearly as far as we had been led to believe. Although I would have to compliment him on the dental. Two kids needing braces for years on end and only a couple of twenty dollar co-pays, that truly was commendable. I would have to give him credit for the dental plan. But I would tell Mr. Graham what for in the rest of the meeting. Right in front of the rest of the staff. And then I would take the staff with me and start a rival company that would soon become an empire.

But I would need to get the details on how they set up the employer match for the retirement fund because I had to admit, that was a good deal too.

Laura could stay home then. She wouldn't need to go back to work. I would make so much more as the head of the newest rival firm in town. She could just go to her yoga class and get even more toned. We could be the sort of empty-nesters who found renewed passion. We could put in a hot tub in the yard. Or a sauna. Something with a little ventilation or maybe an emergency call button. I always thought I might get trapped in one of those things and literally sweat to death. Maybe they made them with an escape hatch. I would get one as long as it had an emergency escape hatch and a button like they had in cars that would auto-dial the emergency services. I'd put it in next to the deck so we could walk right out on it. Maybe a few throw rugs outside to keep the wet feet off the new stain. Our children would come home from college amazed by our transformation. My near death experience would make me into a rakish, devil-may-care, take-no-prisoners, new man. And I would provide them ongoing health coverage under my new corporate empire plan. Because, I had to admit, the fact that I could keep them on my policy at Graham and Graham until they were twenty-five as long as they were enrolled in school fulltime was a very good deal.

Laura would have plenty of time to write my obit for the regular newspaper and for the class notes. 'Laura '79 wrote in with the sad news that her husband Alan, passed away peacefully after a brave battle with malaria acquired during an overseas trip promoting his wildly successful accounting firm start-up. The start-up already had buy-out offers from the biggest accounting giants on the East Coast but Laura is going to use the substantial life insurance money to send underprivileged children to higher education, a cause Alan held dear and championed for many years. She fondly recalled packing his Chesterfields into his blazer pocket before this last fateful trip, a habit he took up after a near death experience many years earlier.'

"Us versus them," Jerry muttered.

"What?" I asked.

"Can you believe it? They exude arrogance. The whole lot. The waiting room full of sick people doesn't know any better. I'm surprised some days that I didn't die out there."

"What do you mean it's us versus them?" I asked.

"Didn't you take history in school? Depersonification. The Nazis did it too. The patients are the untermensch. Too stupid to help themselves."

"Jerry, that's a bit much."

He cocked his head at me. "What would you know? You never had anybody run chemo through a plastic box imbedded in your chest for convenience since all your veins had fried by then. You become the old guy in room 4. The dialysis patient. The pneumonia in room 3. The chest pain. You think I didn't have some knowledge about my delicate condition at that point? I heard what they said about me. I think they are all afraid of their own mortality."

"How so?"

"Depersonification. Patients get sick. Patients die. Patients have complications. Patients are the guy in room 4. Doctors are not the patients. Nurses are not the patients. If us isn't them then us won't have them's problems. It defies logic. Although that kind of logic defies reason."

"Jerry, I don't know if it's possible but my head actually hurts now. I don't normally go to meetings for fun, do you have any better ideas to pass the time?"

He grinned widely.

"Other than the nurses' locker room," I said.

"The executive meeting."

"Give me one good reason."

"Mayhem."

"In a meeting?"

"We could cause it."

"How do you know when this meeting is, anyways?"

"The director mentioned it. Weren't you paying attention? Keep your ears open. We'll follow her. The hostile takeover, the new group, it might be interesting."

They were all seated around an open rectangle of tables. The various chair people of the hospital departments, a few secretaries interspersed; the room buzzed with chatter while everyone waited for the call to order. Some attendees were in suits and clearly had dressed for the occasion. Others were in scrubs, looking at watches, silencing pagers and looking for all the world that they wanted to be elsewhere.

"Good afternoon, everyone." The speaker was a wiry, white haired man with a bow tie and white coat. "For those who may not know me, I'm Dr. Landers, the president of the medical staff. We are two minutes past our allotted time so please take your seats. We have a great deal to cover this afternoon including a presentation on the hospital's financial standing from our CEO, Ms. Belle Evans."

Ears perked up around the table.

Landers adjusted his tie and continued. "I'd like to begin by looking at patient satisfaction scores. We compare it by month and by quarter. As you all know, this is published data and we would like to present this data to the public in a positive fashion. However, certain departments continue to pull down our scores, namely the emergency department and the outpatient psychiatric clinic."

"Is there a difference between the two?" asked one of the doctors across the table.

"Good one, James. Anyhow, perhaps Dr. Williams from the department of psychiatry could address these concerns first."

Dr. Williams was chewing a mouthful of asparagus when he looked up. He quickly speared another spear and popped it in his mouth. He gestured across the room with his now empty fork at the ER director.

Jerry chuckled. "What a cop-out."

"Very well then, perhaps we can start with the emergency department."

The director put down her coffee cup. She wore the same scrubs she had started her shift in and she looked dog-tired. "I have patient satisfaction plaques of ninety-ninth percentile hanging in my office right now. That's where we scored for the last four years until the hospital went with the new survey company."

The nursing director spoke up. "No, you don't. They aren't hanging there. We had to take those down when they took out the dry wall for the new wiring."

Jerry was twiddling with a paperclip and testing its degree of spring.

The director rolled her eyes and continued. "We see up to seven thousand patients a month some months. Does anyone in this room know how many surveys they send out?"

"If this is going to be a rail against the survey company I don't think this is the venue," began Landers.

"One thousand," continued the director. "And how many surveys do you think we have returned?"

"The survey methods are quite solid. We aren't here to question that," said Landers.

"But we did all go to college, and then some of us went on to higher education, if I'm not mistaken, correct? And at some point that included a statistics course or even two? I took two stats classes so I know sometimes this can be intimidating. Don't worry. It's just math. Stay with me."

Landers looked like he was about to cut her off but thought better of it as the room began to rumble.

"We usually get about twenty to thirty surveys back per month. This month we've gotten back twelve. Far less than one percent. A pathetically small sample size that is not even randomized. The only upside I can see to the pathetic sample size is that I have time to personally go through each survey and review the chart. Which I do, on all of them. And today I brought a few."

"Again, may I remind you we are not here to indict the survey. We are here to discuss ways to bring up the scores and project good numbers to the public."

"Then why is the survey company sending surveys to psychotic people and those under arrest? If the outpatient psych clinic has bad scores, I'm sure the ER is worse. Just take the psych clinic cases and add on 'under arrest, beaten up, strung out on meth, doc wouldn't refill my methadone' and go from there. Here's one lady we surveyed. She gave us all 'very poor' across the board but then made some written comments. I quote. 'They wanted a urine sample but I know better. They were just trying to get me pregnant so that I wouldn't tell the CIA that the devil was in the parking meter. They are all terrible at St. Augustine's.'"

"There is no need to be dramatic. I'm sure they aren't all from crazy people," said Landers. He shook a forkful of asparagus for effect.

"Actually, you'd be surprised. A lot of crazy people have an axe to grind, plenty of free time and they love to write. The sane people, at least the ones who come to this ER, are smart enough to give registration a fake address so that we can't bill them so guess where your survey goes. Here's another one, I can take the blame for this one since I happened to see the patient. He wanted to sue a grocery store because he claimed they sold him a six pack of bottled water that was full of bleach instead. He was adamant that they were out to get him, personally. He brought in a bottled water six pack where clearly all six bottles had been opened and refilled. Security had to escort him out because he refused to leave until I tested the bleach levels in the water and talked to that lawyer he saw on TV. And no, I didn't do that. So that column about how well the doctor responded to his needs, not so hot."

Jerry turned to me. "I thought this meeting would have something to do with medicine."

The rest of the room was grumbling. Apparently no one thought much of the surveys.

"Do you know what the happy patients do? The ones who are satisfied? Maybe we saved someone's life or maybe we just stitched up their cut finger and made their day a little better? Usually they don't do anything. They just go on with their day. But sometimes they send thank you cards." She held up a handful of greeting cards. "I don't frankly care what your numbers say. I know what the patients say."

Dr. Landers whispered something to the secretary taking notes and then looked at his watch. "Look at the time! Thank you for those anecdotes and insights. We are out of time on this topic so we will need to table this discussion until the next month."

A groundswell of murmuring from around the table increased.

Across the table, the psychiatrist swallowed his mouthful of pulverized asparagus with relief. He had been chewing energetically the entire time the director was speaking.

"Barb, please make a note that we will revisit sample size as an issue with the survey. I would like to welcome Ms. Belle Evans, CEO of St. Augustine's, to present the latest financial numbers for the hospital."

Jerry grimaced. "I may not be pretty, but at least I look my age. She looks like she got stretched on a drying rack."

I had to agree with him. The CEO looked like, as they say, she had had "work" done. She was probably in her fifties, had a stocky build and a pouf of newscaster hair swept back from her head. She wore one of those necklaces with really large beads that I had never liked let alone understood until my wife pointed out that they were designed to cover up neck wrinkles. Actually she had called them "wattle distracters" and explained to me exactly what turkey neck was. Fortunately I had the presence of mind to tell her that she had not the slightest bit of turkey neck and would never need to cover up her wattle, that is, the wattle that she didn't have. It had been a near miss because she had developed just a little bit of jowls in the last two years, not that I would have ever pointed that out. But at least I had learned before it was too late to never buy her one of those sorts of necklaces. I squinted at the CEO, trying to square up her neck and her face. Maybe they did surgical enhancements in a two part deal, first the face as a priority and then the neck the following year? Kind of like getting one knee replaced at a time. I knew a guy at work who had gone through that. I asked him why he didn't get them both done at the same time if he knew he was going to need it and then I felt pretty dumb when he pointed out that you can't limp on both legs at the same time.

"It is a pleasure to be here," she said. "Despite challenging economic times, I am happy to announce that for this fiscal year St. Augustine's is fully in the black."

Every head in the room turned toward her with varying expressions of complete disbelief.

She smiled through her veneers, pleased to have garnered everyone's attention. Her lips looked out of context, like two slabs of bubble gum stuck on her face. What was that stuff women had injected? Laura had told me about somebody that got it done and it scarred and turned lumpy. Shark cartilage? Collagen?

"As you all know, we serve a very under-insured population. Many of our patients, in fact greater than eighty-five percent, have Medicaid. Up until recently, that was a tremendous liability. Some institutions in town had gone so far as to try and screen out so-called undesirable insurance classes. Fortunately, we did not pursue such a course for that would have been in contradiction with our values we follow as a hospital founded by the Sisters of Charity."

"Can we find a nun to rap her knuckles for wearing too much make up?" Jerry asked me.

"That's not all make up. I think those are fake lips," I replied.

"Really? Like wax?" Jerry was incredulous.

"No, injected with fillers. My wife told me about this sort of thing."

"Your wife doesn't have them does she?"

"Of course not," I said.

"Since we have stuck to our mission of providing charitable care for all patients, irrespective of insurance status, we have been recognized by the state legislature for this work to the tune of a large tax reimbursement," she said.

One of the white coats sitting in front of me rolled his eyes and turned to the director. "This is the only hospital in Chicago that can't figure out some way to offload the Medicaid patients. Nobody else wants to come here."

Belle turned her smile our way.

"There are many other programs at work that have trimmed the budget. It's not merely the tax incentive. Our pathways to excellence initiatives this year have shown substantial savings in staff salaries and benefits."

The director turned to the white coat next to her. "So that's what it was called when they fired my administrative assistant and stopped funding continuing education for the nurses in the ER. I feel so much better now knowing that it was done on the pathway to excellence. We now have an entire group of new hires in nurses who will probably never be trauma-certified. That is just," she paused for effect, "excellent."

Landers frowned from his end of the conference room, unable to quite catch the conversation.

I turned to Jerry. "Ready with those paperclips?"

"I don't know where to aim first."

"With our new advertising push into the suburbs," the CEO went on.

"Is that why you decided to die here? Was it the advertising push?" Jerry asked.

"Shut up," I hissed. "Besides, I'm only half-dead, right?"

"We stand to really make inroads into the more lucrative markets which will of course support the heart of our mission, which is caring for those in need."

The director sighed. "More boob jobs in the burbs and then the ER won't need to hold a bake sale to fund the next cardiac arrest that rolls through the door."

Landers glared from his end of the table. Apparently he heard that one.

"Doctor, that was quite uncalled for. I'm sure you are feeling sensitive what with the corporate staffing changes occurring in the emergency department, but in this economy we have to look at every avenue to remain competitive."

The director pushed her lunch plate forward. "The one thing I have noticed with this economy is that as long as you say 'in this economy' at the start of a sentence, you can justify almost anything. For the record, Barb," she turned and smiled at the secretary typing furiously on her laptop next to Landers. "For the record, I am not feeling sensitive. I am feeling quite relieved personally and I look forward to working in arguably saner if not greener pastures but this group," she gestured in a sweep around the room, "all of you should have some trepidation about the incoming staff to the emergency department."

An old man in a white coat spoke up for the first time. "But isn't most of the staff staying on in the emergency department? We were told the only changes were in the consolidation of the other Sisters of Charity hospitals and the leadership structure."

The director laughed and shook her head. The afternoon light through the blinds was intensifying over her shoulder and the men on the opposite side of the table were squinting.

"Dr. Moss, only one physician from the current group is staying and he is only staying on part-time out of a sense of obligation to the patients and because he doesn't have the emergency medicine certification to work elsewhere. Dr. Manns, as you recall, is grandfathered in to work here under his family practice license but can't get hired with that elsewhere in the city."

The room erupted into angry chatter. Apparently Dr. Manns was a nice enough guy but he didn't know an appendix from a hole in the ground. At the other end of the table, I watched the CEO drum her fingers nervously on her blackberry case.

"Aren't you going to stay?" asked the elder Dr. Moss.

"Certainly not," replied the director. "The contract offered substandard malpractice insurance and a substantial pay cut. Frankly, it was one of the weakest offers I have seen not only in this city but in this region. As I said, I am moving on to at least saner pastures, if not greener."

Belle was fuming. "That is not in the least accurate. They came back with a very different offer after receiving all of your helpful feedback. I don't know why anyone wouldn't take the second offer. The reimbursement is excellent and the malpractice coverage is very standard."

"Because the first offer was so bad it led me to think the new management is one of several things. Disingenuous, incompetent, or underfunded. They might even be all three but I would rather not find out personally. And I advised the staff in the ER to be leery of the contract for the same reasons."

Belle frowned. "This is not the place for insults."

"And when the first contract smelled like a directive from someone to staff the ER with warm bodies until the hospital closes then this is not the hospital for me or any of my doctors."

"I can assure you, there was no such directive. That is an outlandish suggestion and one that I take personal offense at," said Belle.

Conversation in the room rumbled from all corners. Dr. Moss cleared his throat loudly. "If I may get to the point that I'm sure many other people in the room are wondering, just who will be staffing the ER?"

The director grinned. "New grads."

The room resonated with groans.

"Oh, and you might want to ask the nurse manager about her plans to improve the patient to nurse ratio. Or perhaps Ms. Evans has some insight into that along the primrose pathway to excellence? After the last round of cuts it stands at nine to one."

Dr. Moss gave another ahem and some of the rumbling stopped. "What is the usual ratio?"

The director smiled at the manager. "Most people would consider four to one to be a safe ratio for an experienced nurse. The experienced part being key. Nine to one for new nurses is an exercise in lunacy. Or a liability time bomb. Any way you slice it. I only mention this out of a sense of obligation to patient safety and of course to the hospital mission."

Belle Evans looked like she wanted to bite someone. "It is certainly not nine to one. There is a staffing model that I looked at personally that shows a four to one ratio."

"On paper," replied the director, speaking to the rest of the room and ignoring the CEO.

"On paper and in practice" said the CEO.

The nursing manager studiously cut her asparagus spears into smaller and smaller pieces.

Chapter 6

The executive meeting had finished and most of the members had scattered. Two housekeepers packed up the dirty dishes and leftovers from lunch.

"This feels like St. John's" the older woman said.

"What do you mean?" asked the younger woman.

"You too young to know. Right before they closed the hospital. I worked there too. Same job cuts. Worked to the bone to keep up in the last year and then laid off. I'm looking around for something different. You should too. Start looking now while you still have a job," she said, popping a leftover roll in her mouth and falling silent.

"Jerry, what if we're on to something really big?"

"What do you mean?"

"Something doesn't smell right."

"Well, it's not the prettiest hospital on the block but none of them smell that good."

"Jerry, I think they might be cooking the books."

"Why do you think so?"

"Look how shocked everyone was when the CEO said they had made a profit. Nobody believed her. And I don't think I believe her the more I hear about this hospital."

"What's it to you?"

"Maybe that's why I'm here. Maybe that's the purpose behind this whole ridiculous situation. Maybe I'm meant to uncover it and put a stop to it. Maybe I'm here to save St. Augustine's."

"Easy there. Let me tell you something. There is no purpose. Somebody hasn't signed off on me and somebody hasn't made a decision about you. Period. If you think this is the Alan Fries as-in-cheese opera where you find your meaning in life as the unsung hero accountant, I think you have another thing coming. God doesn't take such a personal interest."

"You've been saying that the whole time. How would you know? You talk like you've been dead before."

"Because I've been to war. Because life wasn't so great when I came back from war. But it was good. For Millie and me it was day to day good. And that was enough for me."

"I thought there weren't any atheists in foxholes."

"There might not be. But if God spent his time deciding where every bomb launched by every jackass was going to fall I don't see how he has time to revise his design of the platypus. And he would have a lot of collateral damage to explain. You know what I thought about in the foxholes? Do you really want to know? I thought about the irony that both sides had guys praying to their god to kill the other guy but keep them alive. Crazy doesn't get any crazier than that. And then I spent the rest of the time in the foxhole working on ways to reinforce the foxhole so that my chances of getting killed were less. And that worked because here I am. Well, here I was, I guess I should say. But you get my point."

"No," I said. "I don't get your point. I think the fact that you survived being bombed in a fox hole means that you were meant to live a long life, marry Millie, do all the things you did, heck, go to Cuba even."

"And what does that mean about the other guys?"

"What about the other guys?" I asked.

"The other guys. The guys who died in the foxhole. Condolences to their families because some twisted god meant for them to die, meant for them not to return home to their sweethearts, so it must not be so bad? You need to run with the logic for the full distance if you start down that line of reasoning. I want nothing to do with that. Random chance and preventive strategies is a heckuva lot more comforting to me."

I must admit, I was feeling small at that moment. The last controversy I could think of that I had been embroiled in had involved the subfloor in the bathroom renovation. The contractors ripped up the old tile in the bathroom and the old vinyl in the hall outside. In the process of putting in the new plumbing the subfloor was installed an inch too high in the bathroom. Laura and I both happened to be home when the contractor asked us what kind of a riser we wanted leading into the new bathroom. Laura had taken the charge on that one, hammering him on the details of why the new floor wasn't level when the old floor had been perfectly level. When he blamed it on the subfloor, she even had the presence of mind to point out to him that he had installed the subfloor. Then he turned his attention to me and began a long explanation about how the plumbing pipes had to start out so high and run at a certain angle because of the force of the water. He used the words 'hydrology' and 'hydraulics' in the same sentence and I felt obligated to nod and smile in agreement because as a man I was supposed to know at least something about plumbing.

It wasn't the same thing as fighting to survive in a foxhole, but every time Laura stubbed her toe on the one inch threshold between the hallway and the bathroom she said something choice about my going with the lowest bidder and not knowing the difference between hydraulics and a hole in the ground.

"Look, Jerry. My point is simply that I might want to be productive for as long as I'm stuck here."

"You want to go tabulate something, be my guest. I'll show you where the big shots' offices all are."

"For a man who acts like he is so at peace with being dead you have one heck of an attitude toward the meaning of life."

"What meaning of life?"

"That's what I mean. I get it that you had cancer and were sick for a long time and you're older than me. I'm sure you thought about your death for a long time. But that doesn't make you an authority on it. You haven't died before."

"I died before you did."

"By what, an hour? Give me a break. You know what. I think you're still in denial. Those stages of grief, right? Denial, bargaining, I forget the other ones. You're in denial. And you're taking it out on me by questioning my sense of purpose."

I regretted that as soon as I said it. Because if he asked me I didn't have a sense of purpose. Not a big one. There were still a couple of light switches in my house that I couldn't figure out. We'd lived in the house for nine years and I still didn't know what three of the light switches turned on. I had a sense they must turn other things off and maybe switches down the hall counteracted them. I would be embarrassed to tell Laura how much time I had spent on weekends wandering through the house flipping those three on and off.

And if I didn't figure it out, she certainly wasn't going to. She had no interest in it. How could she sell the house if she couldn't tell prospective buyers what each light switch did?

"I want to see my wife again."

"I can relate. But I still think you're grasping at straws with this meaning of life thing." said Jerry.

"I'm still figuring out my purpose."

"That should have been in your college application essay. Not in your argument today."

"For someone who likes to tear things down I haven't heard you offer many solutions."

"There isn't one. Life goes on for a period of time and then you're dead. That's the way it goes whether you have a purpose or not," Jerry said.

"Didn't you get any counseling when they told you it was terminal?" I asked.

"That was the worst. Those are some strange folks. They're worse than the evangelists. The people in the emergency room actually helped me through it. If something was a crappy deal they weren't going to sugarcoat it. But the counselors, what in the world makes someone go into grief counseling? They either have an issue with death to work out or they are just morbidly curious. Palliative care. The ultimate sugar coaters. They had me pegged as a sad old man the minute they opened my chart. I read some of it, my chart, that is. I got labeled a difficult patient. Thank goodness. I don't need to welcome the reaper grinning like a sheep, doped up on acceptance, methadone, and some half-baked notion of God's plan. They kept telling me I was in denial. What a bunch of crap. I was the one with the dialysis catheter and the chemo port and the pain. I wasn't in denial over any of it, I was perfectly aware of all of it. I tried to stay half in the bag on Jack Daniels is more like it, it worked better than their prescriptions and it didn't make me constipated."

"But you were on dialysis. Doesn't alcohol make your blood thinner then?"

"You bet, Cheese. And I was terribly concerned I might bleed to death before cancer had a chance to get me. You know, if you make it to eighty, you get a list of things that probably won't kill you. And at that point alcohol and smoking are pretty safe. Something else will get you first. They even wanted me to take anti-depressants. Me. In that condition. As if another pill was going to make me feel better about my situation and look at the positive side of cancer. I finally took the prescription but I never filled it because I got sick of talking to the oncologist about it."

"Maybe you were depressed," I said.

"I wasn't depressed. I was in a lousy situation that wasn't that unusual to be in at my age. Our society has made everything into a condition. I don't know why we do it, if it's so the drug companies can make a pill for it or if people are just uncomfortable with reality. Losing Millie and then getting sick were two crappy kicks in the gut. Being down about something or being ticked off about something doesn't mean you need to take a pill. Was I supposed to be happy about it? Of course not, they would say. Am I supposed to take it like just another event in the day? The sky is blue, I lost my pen, I won five bucks in the scratch off, I got cancer? No, of course not, they would say. We understand how important this is to you. This is a life event. No, it's not, I would tell them. Losing Millie was a life event. Getting cancer is just a pain in the ass. And then we would be right back to where we started and they would tell me I was depressed. Bunch of tree-hugging pole smokers. Jack Daniels would at least help me forget about it for a while. And it tastes good."

"Do you believe in God?"

Jerry looked off down the hall as we walked and didn't answer for a while. There were a few people passing us, no eye contact of course, which was unnerving.

"Jerry?" I said.

"I believe that when I leave this place, I am going to see Millie standing right in front of me. And frankly I hope the big bearded guy doesn't get in the way of our conversation because we will have a lot of catching up to do. That's what kept me going for the last ten years. Not talking to him. I don't have much to say to him that he would want to hear. Talking to Millie."

"Did you have children?"

"We had a son."

"Where is he now?"

"He got killed in Vietnam. So he's in Arlington. If you want to be technical about it."

It was my turn to be silent as we walked down the hall.

"You think you'll see him too?" I finally asked.

"I imagine so. That will be tough. We didn't talk much the past couple of years," Jerry said, as if it had been yesterday.

"You ever meet that nurse's kids? Did she ever bring them to the hospital?" I asked.

"True's kids? No, never met them. She showed me pictures a couple of times, when there was a lull in the ER. She has her hands full. Her ex husband moved to another state, California somewhere I think. Four boys."

"She keeps coming to work. To this crazy place. She has a sense of purpose."

"She has bills to pay. I'm sure if she won the lottery she might do something else with her time. But if you're asking me if she's a good nurse then yes, of course she is."

"What's wrong with having purpose?" I asked.

"Look, Cheese, you know what happens when you try to plan too much? Something will wrench up the works. Did I tell you about PFC Brown?"

"I don't think so."

"He got left at a guard post alone for three days."

I shuddered. "In WWII?"

"No, in Fort Riley, Kansas. It was after he came home and he was in the National Guard just doing the annual training in the summer."

I waited for how Jerry was going to use this to explain his views on God.

"He was on base and assigned to a guard post with another guy. And they had a vehicle and a case of c-rats and water. He had all his gear so it wasn't that bad. But the other guy took the vehicle in to post because he was feeling sick. He drove himself to the aid station. Turns out he was really sick because they kept him there for three days.

Well in the meantime, another unit had locked the gate on that road. That was the only reason they had a guard post there was that there was a gate to the outside and since it was training and they were doing some live fire exercises they didn't want just anybody driving around back there.

So PFC Brown has no traffic going by and it was just peaceful. He had enough food.

He was a pretty resourceful guy. From the country. Somehow he started to try and tame this skunk that kept coming into the camp. He left food out for it and he was very quiet and he said it got to the point on the end of the second day that the skunk would come into the building and take a piece of bread and eat it without acting nervous."

"Why was he trying to tame a skunk?" I asked.

"To see if he could. Why not? Anyways, his buddy wakes up at the hospital, kind of comes around and is doing better and tells his nurse that he has to go pick up his friend. Well, she thought he was delirious. It was a training session so they weren't keeping close tabs on everything. They talk to him some more and do an accountability check and then the rest of the idiots in the poor bastard's chain of command realize that they did indeed leave him out there.

Brown didn't mind too much. He was still getting paid for his time whether he spent it working or playing with the skunk. But he has been out there for five days before his buddy drove in and all he really wanted was a shower. A group of four or five guys drive out to the guard post. It was about seven miles so it wasn't like Brown would just walk in and ask for help. When they got there, Brown was inside and he was trying to feed the skunk again so he was really close to it.

Well, the noise of the vehicle and the other guys spooked the skunk and just as the whole group walked into the building, the skunk sprayed. And this little guy, he got everybody."

I was enjoying the story as much as could be expected but I didn't see where Jerry was going with it. "Is the moral to not feed the wildlife?" I asked.

"I'm not done yet," said Jerry. "Remember how I said the only thing that PFC Brown really wanted was to take a shower? This was the army. You didn't just haul five guys back onto the main post who were sprayed by a skunk and get everything contaminated. They had to bring field showers out to them and set up a system to get them all clean before they would let anyone back. You know what they use to neutralize skunk spray, right?"

"Can't say that I do."

Jerry shook his head. "How did you survive this long?"

I glared at him.

"Never mind. Bad play on words. You use tomato juice. And hydrogen peroxide helps too. So the first shower that PFC Brown gets, having been out there for over a week at this point, having been rescued by these numbnuts, the first shower he gets is tomato juice and hydrogen peroxide."

"Did the skunk ever come back?"

"Nah. He ran off into the woods after he sprayed and that was the last they ever saw of him. And to top it all off, they had to spend another six hours out at the guard post waiting for the tomato juice and everything else to get delivered and then the field showers had to get packed back up."

"Jerry, I hate to ask, because it was a good story, but what is your point?"

"My point? My point is to be careful what you wish for. That's my only point. You can't plan too much."

"I probably wouldn't have tried to tame the skunk."

"That's your other problem. You worry too much. If you knew that the worst thing that could happen was that you might need a tomato juice bath, why wouldn't you give it a try? Especially if you got the critter to trust you enough where it would only spray other people. That would be handy."

Chapter 7

It wasn't much farther down the main hall. The carpet changed from threadbare to plush through a big wooden door and the smiling receptionist looked right past us. There was a tall poster on an easel of one of St. Augustine's latest advertisements. Belle Evans' photoshopped head with the shark-cartilage lips smiled in the middle of it, under their latest mission statement on compassion.

"Bigwig has the corner office. I'm going back to the ER to watch the next crazy piss on the wall."

"Will you come get me in an hour?"

"Will do." And with that he was gone and I was alone for the first time all day. Alone except for the living, that is. I stood outside the office and heard voices behind the polished mahogany door. I leaned in closer. Probably a laminate mahogany. Couldn't risk opening and closing it. I grit my teeth and walked through it. Of all the things I daydreamed about as a kid: flying, being invisible, making wishes that all my next wishes would come true to trick the genie, walking through walls was never one of them. Hadn't really thought of it before. Being invisible, definitely. But I was tired of it already. And walking through walls, or in this case, walking through a solid door, just confirmed the thing I didn't want to think about. That I was at least half dead.

The CEO was alone in the office on the phone. I was much closer than I had been in the meeting. Bigwig wasn't a bad name for her, I thought. She looked like she was wearing a hairpiece. Somewhere north of fifty, she had embarked on a youth campaign that had nipped and botoxed her into the same expressionless face that was on every evening news show, but without quite the same results. Airbrushed on the poster, she looked worse. Alone in her office, talking on her blackberry, at least her face was moving.

"Frank? It's Belle. Oh, doing fine thank you. This is my private phone. I need to talk a few numbers with you. You have a moment? Good. Yes, it's about your nursing home patients. Yes, the numbers are fine for the last six months. But I need you to increase it for the next eighteen months. The state tax credit for Medicaid is going to be continued for the next fiscal year. I need you to admit at least another 200 patients a month. Very win-win. But nobody too high maintenance. My nursing ratios on the floors are so tight as it is I can't be putting in patients with real needs."

I was busy searching the room for a spare pad of paper and something to write with when I realized it might distract her if office objects started to float.

"No it's not the reimbursement per patient. The reimbursement is still abysmal. It's the numbers at the end of the fiscal year. Quantity is the game. We pulled in fifty seven million dollars from the state last year. This year we stand to pull in something in the eighties if you can meet those targets. Yes. Exactly. Of course I'm discreet. It's all in the coding. You document therapy, therapy happened. But I have an idea of a way we might expand this."

The phone crackled on the other end.

"More risk and a higher percentage are perfectly reasonable. I trust your piece of the fifty-seven million was adequate. Good. I wondered if you know a surgeon and perhaps a cardiologist who are equally discreet? You know where I'm going right? The odd gallbladder, hip replacement, cardiac stent or so? But Frank, you'll have to do a lot more legwork on these. We can't have family members start questioning why procedures are getting done. You will need to be more involved in patient selection. No hurry for this month but if we could start before the next fiscal year I would appreciate it."

The conversation wrapped up in chit chat and I had at least forty-five minutes before Jerry would be coming back.

The CEO left with her blackberry and locked her door behind her. Good, I thought, done for the day. No problems with a few floating files. I sat down in the leather chair and toggled the mouse. The computer was still on. It was still on and the CEO was still logged in. This had to be a stroke of luck. I doubted she would usually leave her computer unsecured. I clicked on the office icon and began reading through her emails. I glanced at the clock and began hitting print on all the emails between the CEO and this Dr. Lazarus. Next there were some spreadsheets.

The time flew and I didn't even realize how late Jerry was in getting back until he reappeared through the door.

"Sorry I'm late."

"It's OK. I've found a gold mine in the meantime. What kept you?"

"Big case in the ER. I had to stay and watch."

"Trauma?"

"No, much better. Drama. Big lady comes in with the police. She's under arrest. And drunk as a skunk and not happy. She beat somebody else up but she's got a few bumps and bruises so they bring her here. Manage to get her into a hospital gown and she's got it on proper, open in the back, and she's still cursing up a storm. The new security guard is doing the bob and weave to keep her from flying out the door. Keeps saying, just get in the bed, just try to relax. Well, she gets into his face, he puts his hands on both her shoulders and grabs the hospital gown. She takes a step back and dodges around him and runs. Full starkers and not a pretty sight, straight past the mural they keep griping about, into the double doors and wham, head on crash and falls back to the floor out cold. Those doors don't open unless you push the button on the wall, you know. But the best part..."

"Is there a best part?"

"The best part is the new security guard is standing there the whole time after she bolts, just holding the hospital gown and kind of looking behind it, looking around the room as if he can't figure out where she went. Newbies. True had to call him to get him to snap out of it and come peel the lady off the floor."

"True?"

"You know. Garden hose. The one that has the thing with the newbie doc."

"Got it." I was smiling in spite of myself at Jerry's story.

"Reminds me of a guy I used to work with. We were all in South Korea for a conference, it was a tele-com thing. There was a lot going on in town and the hotels were booked. Not a lot of hotels to choose from there and man, they are into the quickie hotels."

"Quickie hotels?" I asked.

"Hotels for a quickie. People live with so many relatives there isn't much privacy. Married couples go to these more often than anybody else. Mirrors on the ceiling. Pretty typical. And that's where we were staying, this place with mirrors on the ceiling. Anyways, we all went out and had some drinks and got in late. Frank, this guy, he was a big drinker and he really tied it on that night. Well, I was down in the lobby the next morning at their little continental coffee bar, not much to speak of but this was before you could get coffee in your room and all the stuff you get now. Frank comes running into the lobby completely naked screaming that he was attacked by a naked fat guy in his room. You need to understand, Frank was younger than me and he had been to Vietnam and he was a little shook up just being in Asia to begin with. Probably not the best guy for that trip."

"But Koreans and Vietnamese are different," I said.

"Do you think I don't know that, Cheese? It didn't make a difference to Frank. He had his guard up. They threw him a towel from the desk and I go over and talk to him and some little security guard who looked like he was twelve shows up and we all head back to Frank's room. Doors wide open. Bed's a mess. Security guard asks him where the other guy was and Frank is shouting that he was on top of him. Says he woke up and some fat naked guy was on top of him. I've got the same kind of room with the mirror on the ceiling. I point at it to Frank and ask him if the guy was up there.

He's quiet for a minute and he keeps looking at the bed and at the ceiling and then he kind of tightens the towel around his waist and starts laughing. 'Oh shit, it was me,' he says. The security guy now thinks he's completely crazy if he didn't already and he doesn't really speak enough English to understand what's going on and Frank falls back on the bed and looks up at the ceiling and is laughing even harder, so hard he can't even get the words out. So I tipped the guard a few bucks and told him it was OK and sat there for a while with Frank. He'd passed out drunk in his bed, saw himself in the mirror when he woke up, and panicked. We laughed about that for years. He never did lose any of the weight. You'd think that might have encouraged him."

Jerry was grinning from ear to ear and shaking his head in amazement, chuckling. He finally looked back at me.

"So," he said.

"So?" I said.

"So what's your gold mine?"

"It's huge. Are you ready?"

For once, he looked interested. "Shoot."

"The CEO double-counted the tax incentive."

"In layman's terms that make it actually interesting?"

"She cooked the books."

"Making the place look more profitable than it is?" Jerry asked.

"Exactly. Two years ago the board of directors fired the old CEO and gave Belle Evans a directive to decrease the amount of patients this hospital saw. So she came in as your typical slash and burn replacement. She cut services, fired from the middle on down, changed nurse to patient ratios, closed portions of the hospital and saved a lot of money. At the same time they increased their advertising in the suburbs to get a different insurance class to come to St. Augustine's.

At the same time, the state passed legislation giving a big tax incentive to hospitals taking care of Medicaid patients, the lowest reimbursement class. It's cyclical. The state did the same thing about ten years ago before St. John's closed. It's a pump and dump for the hospital CEO. After St. John's closed, the Medicaid volume surged here so they stood to profit from this. That year

St. Augustine's was running a deficit of eighty-three million dollars. The tax reimbursement was fifty-seven million. Helpful, but it only plugged the hemorrhage. Didn't cure it."

Jerry frowned. "You sound like you have a talent for accounting. So far sounds shitty but legit."

"So far," I said. "But she double counts the incentive as a refund and income. Her chief financial officer looks culpable in the emails I read. So now the hospital made one-hundred and fourteen million, which turns the deficit into a profit of twenty-two million dollars."

"But won't that come out next year? Where did they come up with the money if the real balance sheet is twenty-six million in the red?"

"It's bound to come out eventually. They pulled the money out of the endowment. She's probably hoping the endowment will recover it when the stock market improves. But there's even more. She took a five million dollar bonus this year from the board of directors due to putting the hospital in the black."

"That may be true this year, " Jerry said, "but next year she'll be in the clink for fraud so what's her purpose?"

"Bigger things. I overheard a conversation she had with a doctor who by the sounds of it runs a bunch of nursing homes. He's been sending patients to St. Augustine's this past fiscal year who are almost vegetables and they bill Medicaid for physical therapy and a bunch of things they don't need. Sounds like he doesn't even send in people who really need treatment because it would be too time-consuming on this end. The CEO even told him not to send complicated cases because she doesn't staff enough nurses on the floors to take care of people with real needs."

Jerry listened quietly. "Did you catch his name?"

"Frank Laz-something. His last name is in some of the emails."

Jerry frowned.

"The CEO wants him to send even more patients this year and is on the lookout for surgeons and other specialists to do procedures and further bilk Medicaid. It sounds like she wants to get procedures done whether they need them or not as long as they technically qualify. And she's promising him a cut of the profits if he does. I got so mad listening to this I wanted to grab the blackberry out her hand and wing it at her head."

Jerry had his head down, looking at the papers.

"Jerry, forget what I said about purpose before and all that. I don't even care if this if why I'm stuck here. I don't care if it gets me back or not. This is wrong and we have to stop it."

Jerry was silent, poring over the paperwork on the expansive desk.

"Jerry?"

He looked up with a firmly set jaw and a hard stare. "Millie, my wife, was in a nursing home for the last year of her life. She had lymphoma. It was in her bones and she had a couple of fractures. We had Medicaid for her in the end. She was in and out of the hospital a dozen times that year, right before St. John's closed. None of it made any sense to me at the time. They would admit her to St. John's for some orthopedic surgeon to see her. They recommended a hip replacement even though her oncologist told her not to get one, that the tumors were too advanced and she wouldn't be able to do the follow up therapy. Then I couldn't get her admitted anywhere when she had a fever and probably pneumonia. I don't know who the CEO was at the time but Frank Lazarus was her doctor."

I was stunned silent.

"She told me about another lady in the home. This lady was over a hundred, I think a hundred and three when she died. She had Alzheimer's so she would forget who you were but she got around on her own with a walker. She fell and broke her hip and got moved into Millie's wing. She was her roommate for just a few days. Some doctor was pushing for her to get hip surgery. Her power of attorney was a nun, kind of a modern nun though, no habit, just dressed plain. And she was a smart lady. Millie overheard them arguing. The doctor was pushing for surgery and the nun was explaining that the old lady's Alzheimer's was so bad that she wouldn't understand why she was doing the physical rehab, you know, having to get up and walk and all that after the surgery. It's a lot of pain. She couldn't remember from day to day anyway. So doing physical therapy would have been like torture. This nun had it all figured out and she didn't back down from the surgeon. And aside from the pain, there was the risk of surgery, anesthesia, and infection, all of it. The nun wanted her to just be on bed rest and get medication for pain and they would see if her hip healed or not. The lady was over a hundred. Back and forth. Millie was impressed by the nun because this guy, this other doctor, he really was pushing for it. Now it makes sense."

"Did she have the surgery?" I asked.

"No, they wouldn't sign off on the consent."

"What happened to her?" I asked.

"She died in her sleep a week later. Alan, do we have enough to get these people?"

"Enough what?" I stammered.

"Enough evidence. Enough crap to give the board of directors or the media or someone who will listen."

"Yes we do. Emails, handwritten notes, accounting records. It's all there. I even forgot to add one more thing."

"What's that?"

"Belle Evans has a golden parachute for eleven million dollars if she lasts three years as CEO."

Jerry began to pack all the papers on the desk into a spare file folder. "We need to get back to the ER."

"Why the ER?"

"To make sure nobody signs my death certificate any time soon."

Chapter 8

True was back for the swing shift and arrived at the ER in a foul mood. Jerry and I came through the double doors behind her. She would have knocked me over with her thermos and backpack if I had been flesh and blood.

"Damn nuns."

"Easy, killer. You don't want to burn for all eternity do you," said Alvarez.

"Do you know I woke up an hour early just to go to a conference with those old bats and basically got accused of being an alcoholic? Jake is in second grade this year and happened to mention to his teacher that his mommy has beer with breakfast. OK, people have a beer with dinner after work, right? Breakfast is my dinner. I work the night shift. How hard is that to understand? But Mrs. Miller, we have seen you come through the car circle in the afternoon with your pajamas on and let's just say, not looking your best. Drinking all day in your pajamas while your kids are at school is just not conducive to a good home environment. They. Actually. Said. That. Hello, I've been sleeping all day while the kids are at school. And if I look like crap it's because I didn't get enough sleep. And it's Ms. Miller since the Mr. left town to find himself. I tried to explain this to these ladies and they looked at me like I had three heads. Work at night and sleep in the day.

Simple. Except that people do things at ten in the morning like run their snow blower and that wakes up the night shift worker. Me! And then I look like crap by three in the afternoon," True was fuming.

"Did they get it in the end?" Alvarez asked?

"Not really. They ended the conference with a bunch of smarmy, if you need any help don't hesitate to ask and perhaps if you would forgo the beer with breakfast your day would go smoother. And I reminded them it's not my day it's my night."

"So why do you have your kids in Catholic school again?"

"For the moral grounding," True replied. "And don't even start. I'm going to have to have my beer in the car on the way home from work so they won't see me."

Alvarez raised an eyebrow.

"Kidding!" said True.

"Jake didn't tell them about the time you followed him home on the beach because his shoes blinked did he?" asked Alvarez.

"No. I think he was too young at the time to remember it exactly."

Maglio turned his chair to join the conversation. "Why were you following the blinking shoes exactly?"

"It was dark on the beach," True hedged.

"And?"

"And some alcohol was involved."

"I see…."

"Come off it Maglio. Like you never got loaded on a beach. We were in Michigan at a summer cottage and all these little places are built on cliffs and you have to take stairs to get up and down to the beach. We drove up the road to some friends, had a bit too much to drink, and decided to be responsible and not drive home," said True.

"So the responsible thing was to climb down a cliff in the dark?"

"It was stairs. Not a cliff. Well, the stairs were on the cliff. Anyway, when we got to the bottom it was dark. I mean, really dark. I knew the other cottage and the stairs was about half a mile south. I had some friends with me, we were about five girlfriends, Jake, and another older kid who was about twelve. And Jake was wearing those shoes that blink when you step. It wasn't that we needed him on the beach so much as on the stairs. You need to understand, this was northern Michigan coastline. There were no streetlights, nothing. So we made a game out of it. He climbed a step, then he would jump up and down a couple times and I could tell where the step was."

"Your responsibility as a parent is inspiring," said Maglio.

"Like you would know. You're the one with the vasectomy."

"Ahem," Maglio cleared his throat. "As we so often comment in our line of work, the ability to shoot swimmers does not equate with the ability to be a parent."

"Point taken," said True. "Anyways, it tired him out and when we got to the top of about eighty stairs, we were back at the cottage and he fell asleep."

"So the ladies could keep drinking?" asked Alvarez.

"A little. Yes. Maybe. But that wasn't the point. And we went back the next morning in daylight to get the car. No harm done," said True.

"And Jake doesn't remember leading the drunk ladies down the beach," said Maglio.

"He does not. He remembers leading a parade and he was very proud of himself. And the nuns know nothing about it. I bet they drink behind closed doors any way."

"I would smuggle all kind of stuff under the habit if I wore one," mused Maglio. "And I would definitely pick one of the groups that brew their own beer."

"I thought only the monks did that," said Alvarez.

"They just take credit for it."

The director sat down at the computer next to Maglio. He promptly opened a file on his desk top on the latest treatments for acute coronary syndrome and pretended to read it intently.

She coughed.

He studiously ignored her.

"Maglio."

"Oh, hi. Didn't see you there. Have you read this on the latest accuracy of spiral CT in diagnosing calcium deposits in the coronary arteries?"

She pushed her glasses down her nose, arched her head back and stared down the narrow rims at him. "And the lack of ability to see the softer plaques that are more likely to fragment, travel downstream and cause an acute infarction in patients whose pricey CT gave them a false sense of security? I think I read that. In fact, I think I advised Holy Tino's not to invest in that as a testing strategy. One of the few pieces of advice from me that they actually took. Maglio. Stop stalling. You need to sign this."

"Sign what?"

She pushed the chart toward him.

"Gerald Verne. Lord knows we all loved the guy and Dr. Leak would have loved him too if he met him but the certificate rests with you."

"Why won't Leak do it?"

"At this point I don't care why Leak won't do it. Maybe he broke both arms trying to rescue a girl scout troop and so he can't write; tell yourself that if it makes you feel any better. I do care that I got three different phone calls from administrators asking me what the hold up was today. The joint commission is here, remember? This is a no-brainer, Maglio. Just sign it and put it in campus mail back to medical records today, OK?"

"Is Leak on today?"

"Maglio, what does it matter?"

He called across the ER to the secretary. "Paula, is Leak on call today for general admissions?"

"Sure is," she answered. The cart with the orange buckets and bottled water was still parked by the desk.

"It matters because I am going to admit the biggest trainwreck I can find to him. But yes, I will do the paperwork. Just leave it here."

"Maglio."

"What?"

"I just came from the medical executive committee meeting and I think the CEO wants my head on a pike. Oh wait, I'm already fired. I must have forgot. When is our contract up again? February 1st cannot come too soon. If I have to talk to any one of them in the next twenty-four hours I will lose what's left of my mind. Sign it."

"Is that four hundred pound guy with gangrene still here? That would be a great case for Leak."

"No, I sent him to the ICU before the meeting." She pushed the chart closer to Dr. Maglio.

Jerry practically lunged for it but I waved my hands in his face. "No floating paperwork!" He was already holding the other file next to the back of a chair so the silhouette wouldn't be as obvious. "He won't do it now, just wait until the director leaves and he pushes it off again," I said.

However, Maglio took a pen out of his coat pocket and started thumbing through Jerry's file. "Fine, I'll sign it. But I still think Dr. Leak is an ass." Jerry scanned the desk and seized a reflex hammer. He held it for a moment and then brought it smartly into contact with Dr. Maglio's elbow.

"Yow!" he called. "Who did that?" He spun his chair around and clutched his elbow.

"Dr. Maglio, I have the cardiologist on line two for you regarding room seventeen," said the secretary.

"That's no reason to hit me in the arm."

"Wasn't me."

Jerry deftly slid his file across the table and behind the chair with the other papers. "That's the funny bone all right. Now, who is going to be our whistleblower?"

"Somebody you can trust. You know these guys better than me."

Jerry's gaze fell on True and the intern. "One foot out the door and naïve and ready to save the world. There's our team."

Watching the intern intently flip paperclips toward the charge nurse's coffee mug, I had my doubts. "Jerry, I'm not sure which is worse, the fact that he's spending time playing the paperclip game or the fact that his hand-eye coordination is that bad."

"It's OK. He might be a moron but he thinks he can save the world. As long as he doesn't become a surgeon I could care less about his hand eye coordination. My last dialysis session he was rotating through trying to learn something about the kidney and all he could talk about was the reform of the medical system and how he wants to get plugged in with all the politicos and make it happen. And True, well True, she might be crazy but she loves this place."

"He reminds me of my younger brother."

"Is that a good thing?" asked Jerry.

"No," I said.

"Where do you fall in the Fries tree?"

"I'm the middle brother. Six kids."

"Hand me downs."

"Plenty of hand me downs. Fortunately not too many photos as evidence."

"You'd love those photos now."

"Only because if I'm dead maybe nobody else can see what I'm looking at," I found myself laughing at the absurdity of it all, laughing harder than I probably should.

"Worst hand me down item. What was it?" Jerry asked.

"You really want to talk about this?"

"I'd rather hear you blather than listen to the intern woo a nurse who should have higher aspirations than him. Besides, I'll keep one eye on them and figure out when they get to see the file."

"Turtleneck dickie," I said.

Jerry snorted.

"That was the worst item," I said.

"That doesn't sound like an article of clothing; that sounds like a maneuver best kept behind closed doors."

"Come on Jerry, you know what a dickie is, right?"

"I thought it was one of those fake shirt fronts that women wear to cover up their cleavage."

"Usually. But my mother sewed a lot of our clothes and she made us dickies to wear under these v-neck Christmas sweaters."

"Good God, Cheese, how did you even survive school? Were you a fat kid?"

"No."

"Then why was your mother trying to cover up your cleavage?"

"I didn't have cleavage. I think it was just a sewing project. Anyways, my uncle Joe found out about it one afternoon because we were playing in the garage after church and it was warm in there with the door closed. I must have been about six years old and I'm chasing after my older brother. It got too hot so I took off the itchy sweater and left it on the rear bumper of the car we were running around but I kept on the turtle neck dickie because it was so hard to get that over my neck. My brother didn't care but my uncle Joe came out through the garage, probably to go have a smoke and saw me. Pants, dress shoes, turtleneck dickie.

He had never gotten along well with my mom, his sister. It was a rift over a car that got sold instead of being given to either of them, a rift that just grew a life of its own and kept growing. He asked what the hell I was wearing and I didn't know what it was called so I just said that mom made it.

By the time I came back inside, she was yelling and Uncle Joe was putting on his coat and he wasn't invited back for holidays at our house after that."

"And this reminds you of your younger brother why?"

"It doesn't. But you asked about hand me downs. And I told you the intern reminds me of my younger brother. Full of ideas but no common sense."

"That's perfect though. We need someone who can walk up to the board of directors and hand them the whole file."

"Jerry, how do we even find the board of directors? They don't move around in a big pack. They probably never even come to hospital."

"We get the intern to take it to them. We make it irresistible. We make it romantic."

I snorted. "Jerry, I can't picture you making anything romantic."

"You're prejudiced against old guys. See how you feel when somebody says that to you when you're eighty but not dead. Hell, I'm dead and I still have feelings. And I want to get this little errand out of the way so I can spend some time in the nurse's locker room before I check out of here."

"You'll have eternity to look at women."

"I don't know that. You keep asking me questions like I'm the expert on being dead just because I died four minutes before you. Maybe heaven has a lot of robes and praying and not much else.

It may not even have locker rooms. Maybe its gender separated for all I know."

"I ask questions because you act like the expert on being dead."

"I'm the expert on being in the ER. That's it."

"What should we do with your chart?"

"Shredder box. Put it under some other stuff. And maybe I'm the expert on being old. But not on being sick. I hated being sick. And it didn't give me any practice for being dead, in case you are going to ask. All being sick did was piss me off."

"Who were you pissed off at?"

"There were plenty of people. The people that visited and gave me that look. That look that's half-gloating that it isn't them and half pity which is about the same thing. The people who didn't visit but should have. The insurance salesman who would call and try to get me to put money into an annuity. The other old guys who wanted to talk about their bowels. The other old guys who wanted to talk about old cars. The people who hadn't spent a day in the service who loved to wax poetic about the war as if they had a right to." Jerry harrumphed.

"That covers a lot of ground. Did you get along with anyone before you died?" I asked.

"Of course I did. True, the nurse. My barber. The guy that did the lawn-mowing."

"Anybody close to you?"

Jerry shook his head. "You don't get it. You're too young. They were all gone. The people close to me were already dead. Just a fact of life. And yes, I tried to get out. I would get sick of the four walls. I went to the VFW. I went to the diner. And then I went home and was happy just to be home. On days I wasn't doing something medical. You know, Alan, back in the day I was reading Jules Verne and later Vonnegut and I thought we were going to have jetpacks. I mean genuine strap-it-on and go jet packs to travel everywhere. Colonization of Mars. Missions to Mercury. Vacations to the moon. And what do we have now? Rascals."

"Rascals?" I asked.

"Those motorized chairs people ride around on when they get too fat."

I thought about it for a moment. "Don't some of the people that use them have neurological disorders or something too? It's not just for fat people."

"Alan. I've been around that crowd. Ninety-nine percent are for fat people. Spending time with people my own age involved way too much talking about who had what disease and how everybody's knees hurt. What a newsflash. I'm eighty-seven and my knees hurt. Let me tell you all about it over a cup of coffee. Hell no. Think they would talk about the news? Politics? Debate something? Nope. Or they'd go on and on about their grandkids and what little geniuses they were. No, I was happy enough being home. Alone. The house reminded me of Millie and it was quiet there. I don't know what the future holds for humanity. Frankly I'm happy that it's not my responsibility. But it looks like it's going to be a society of fatties on rascals. Now follow me, they're headed into the break room."

"Who, the fatties?" I asked.

"Our whistleblowers! Aren't you paying attention."

True and the intern sat down at the formica table and waited for the microwave popcorn to cool down. There was a big box in the corner overflowing with holiday decorations. The box next to it had oxygen tubing snaking out the top. The table was littered with leftovers. A spare egg roll here, half a donut of indeterminate age there, extra condiment packets that nobody would ever throw away but that nobody would ever use. The intern poured a cup of coffee and rifled through the packets.

"Mayo, tartar sauce, salt and pepper. Why don't we have creamer and sugar packets by the coffee instead?" the intern asked.

"That would make sense," said True.

"I've never even heard of some of these. Captain D's Special Fish Sauce? Is that place even in business? I've never seen a place like that around here."

"They went out of business about five years ago. So that is a vintage sauce packet."

"Rondo's Secret Sauce. I don't even want to know what that is."

"They're still in business," said True. "And no. You don't"

"Why does everyone save their condiments? I see this in every nursing break room. You get Chinese food, you get fifty little packets of stuff. You sauce up your food in the break room and see a pile of packets. Why add two more sweet and sour packets to the giant pile. It's only stuff that nobody uses. My parents do this in their kitchen. They throw all the packets in the junk drawer and then they get mixed in with the paperclips and the screwdrivers and they puncture and then the soy sauce leaks on everything," the intern despaired.

"Life's mysteries, Olson."

"I can never find cream and sugar."

"Maybe you should learn to drink black coffee," True suggested.

"Never. I already drink bad coffee. And I don't want to taste it any more than I have to."

Jerry was rifling through the condiment packets, muttering to himself.

"It's like gnomes," he said.

"What?" I asked.

"It's like gnomes. One year my wife got a garden gnome. She didn't want to offend the person who gave it to her, happened to be a neighbor who could walk by our house every day if they wanted to, so she put it in the yard. Then her sister saw it and gave her a gnome. By next Christmas we had four more. That was just the beginning. She couldn't stand them. I couldn't either. The only good thing, and I mean the only good thing, that came of her dying, was the yard sale I got to have. I got to sell all the gnomes. Not only did I sell them all, but I dropped the hint that the sight of them made me miss Millie. So nobody ever gave me another one." Jerry had his arms folded across his chest and looked satisfied.

"How does this relate to relish and mustard packets?"

"People see a pile of something and they add to it. Especially if it's in a bucket. They assume they are supposed to. This must be where I put my extra sweet and sour sauce. The Vernes like garden gnomes. Everybody goes to church and stands up and sits down in unison so I should too. Next thing you know you're voting for a dictator."

"I don't think people actually vote for dictators. And that's kind of a stretch to make from a pile of relish packets," I said.

"What do you mean people don't vote for a dictator? They elected Hitler and then he became a dictator," said Jerry. "Dictators have to start out popular to get their power base. And don't get me started about some of our presidents. And the religious wackos. The worst case scenario is when they're both. It's like those TV guys that think the world is going to end but for whatever reason they need donations of cash right up until that date."

"But nobody listens to those guys," I said.

"Of course they do. One of the guys last year had people sending in their whole retirement savings to help buy billboards advertising the day of judgment. Millie and I used to live near a couple like that. They thought it was their duty to help us get saved. Makes me nuts. The idea that some supposedly compassionate god is going to destroy the universe and take some selected souls up to heaven while killing millions of people in the process. And they celebrate that. They look forward to it like it will be a nice neighborhood cook out. And then the judgment day prophecy came and went and however many millions of dollars later, the guy says he miscalculated and the actual day will be next year. So send me another check. Ridiculous. They're lucky I didn't shoot them on my porch the last time they rang the doorbell."

"But that's the fringe element."

"That's what you think. I didn't live in a fringe neighborhood. You wouldn't have known it until they started yammering. How wonderful it will be when the universe gets destroyed. After Millie died they got even more interested in my soul. They had the gall to tell me that I needed to be saved in order to see her again on the day of judgment. Arrogant bastards. They would have been burning people at the stake in an earlier time. I got them to leave me alone eventually."

"Were these the same people that left when you invited them in to watch porn?"

"Nah, they were mild in comparison. No, this crew was worse," Jerry said.

"So how did you get them to leave?" I asked.

"Asked if they had health insurance that covered them for lead poisoning."

"I don't follow you."

"Well, I asked the question while standing on the porch with a shotgun."

"Did they call the police?"

"Not for that. They called the police later because I was mowing the yard in my bathrobe. Complained about indecency. It happened to be a windy day. I think they were mad because I told their kids the world would end based on the Mayan calendar and the kids didn't know who the Mayans were."

"I know who they were but I didn't know they thought the world was going to end."

"End of next year. If you can read the chicken scratch on the rocks the right way. Supposedly. These kids were home schooled so they had their own version of history. Of course if they had gone to the public schools they wouldn't have been taught anything about the Mayans either. Pick your poison. They're all spending too much time in sex ed to learn anything."

"Jerry, the schools aren't that bad,"

"You think they aren't? You should read the newspaper. Anyhow, get ready for the nutjobs to escort their cults down to Machu Picchu in another year. But send cash first. It sounds good right? You can be one of the chosen by joining the club. No responsibility for anything on earth because it's all going to be destroyed anyways. Throw in some catchy songs and pot luck suppers, everyone's smiling, and next thing you know, you've voted for the dictator. And if you don't, it's rather inconvenient because you'll be destroyed by a giant fireball, or thrown in a flaming pit. None of these nutjobs have been to war or they would understand what men do to each other already. We don't need a deity to help out in our destruction. We are doing a great job on our own."

"Did you tell your neighbors that?"

"Something to that effect."

"And what did they think?"

"They called some crank from the Department of Aging to come check on me. I let her in the house just to see what she would do. She looked in the fridge and made notes on the clipboard. I offered to help her inventory by naming all the condiments on the door and apparently that wasn't the purpose of the list. She was concerned I might have vitamin deficiencies and I asked her how that would affect my views on religion. Apparently the neighbors hadn't told her that that was the real reason they had called. My fridge passed. Barely. I wasn't much of a cook after Millie died. But I had enough stuff in there to reassure the social worker. The rest of her notes were on trip hazards. She told me that. I thought she was talking about landmines at first, you know, trip wires and such. But no, apparently the most dangerous thing to an old guy is a throw rug because they cause ninety-nine percent of falls or some such nonsense. I asked her how much money she made per year and she wouldn't tell me. So I asked her how much of my tax money went to pay her salary so she could come to my house and count my throw rugs. That seemed to make her mad and she left. Not long after that I met my neighbors with the shotgun and then they stopped sending anyone over."

"Where did she get the information on throw rugs?" I asked.

"Really Alan? Do I have you worried now?"

"I must admit, you piqued my interest," I said.

"For God's sake. I'm sure the information came from the Department of Throw Rugs. But they might have an industry bias so you can't be sure. Don't you find it a little problematic that some bureaucrat can show up at your house, count your rugs and your pantry stock of soup and then decide whether you can stay in your home?"

"It sounds like they were just checking to see if you needed meals on wheels," I said.

"Oh no, it wasn't that. Neighbors that want their compassionate god to smite you with brimstone don't want you to get a food basket. They want you out of their neighborhood so you stop telling their kids about Mayan human sacrifice."

"I thought you didn't believe in the end of the world stuff."

"I don't think the world is going to end based on the Mayan calendar, no. But the human sacrifice history happened. I was telling the kids something from history," Jerry said. "Something that might sound terrible enough that they would question celebrating the apocalypse instead of acting like happy little robots."

I wasn't going to egg him on. But what if he was on to something. It started early. Putting socks away. That was one of the first things I remember doing as a chore when I was a kid. I was very proud of myself when I figured out how to match my socks. Finding the missing sock in the big laundry basket always made my mother so happy. Or maybe she was just humoring me. But even now, well lately anyways, before all this time at the hospital, I would rearrange my socks. Usually it was on Sunday evening before the work week but sometimes I would do it during the week while Laura was at yoga. Especially when she was at yoga. It kept me from picturing her in those pants limbering up with strangers. Roll the argyles and space them away from the solid pattern socks. I might be spending more time at it than I should.

But I didn't put them in a bucket. I put them in the drawer. It made me think about the bucket list that everybody talked about. Those things you were supposed to have on your bucket list. I guess it referred to when you kicked the bucket, not just any bucket.

I wanted to ask him about the throw rug statistics. I would take stock of our situation when I was home. Getting through a near death experience I wouldn't want to go home, slip on something, and break a leg. That would be my luck. And it was going to change how I set things up for parties on the newly stained deck.

"Jerry, did you have a bucket list?"

"A what?"

"You know, a bucket list. A list of things you had to do before you died. Climb Machu Picchu. See the Mona Lisa. That sort of thing."

"Hmm. I had a bucket list of sorts earlier. But I changed it in the last couple of years to the unbucket list," said Jerry.

"Things you already did?" I asked.

"Things I never wanted to do again."

"How did that work out?"

"Between dialysis and chemo the list kept getting longer. I recommend it. You start to prioritize."

I thought about the hypothermia catheter and realized I had a start. But I couldn't dump anything out of the unbucket, just keep it from getting more full. It seemed like there had to be a better way.

"Like the garden hose," Jerry suggested.

"I was thinking of that," I agreed. "That would go on the list."

"But there's more to it than that. You can unbucket anything. Not living on anything other than the top floor in an apartment building, for example."

"Why?" I asked.

"Why? So nobody drops shoes on your head when you're trying to sleep. Or walks around. Planning, Alan. Planning and don't let them push you around. Not getting a hotel room next to the ice machine. Not making airline reservations with a twenty minute layover at O'Hare so that you're guaranteed to miss your connection. Those things that at the time when you're talking yourself into it you know it's a bad idea. Unbucket. Never again. Don't even start it. Did I ever tell you about the guy whose dog used to crap in my yard?"

"I don't think so."

"Every day. Every day for about two weeks after this pole smoking yahoo moved in. He'd let his dog out and the thing would walk over and leave a big steamer right in my lawn. I saw him do it at least three times and by the time I went to the neighbor's door I must have had a collection of twenty craps. Do you know what he had the nerve to tell me?"

"I can't imagine," I said.

"Rogue dog. He said he had heard that there was a rogue dog in the neighborhood that somebody left off the leash that was crapping in people's yards. Strangely enough not his yard, which I pointed out to him. Strangely enough the dog looked just like his dog. But he's heard that too. He'd heard, like he went to some convention where they were discussing dog crap, he's heard that the rogue dog looked like his dog. I asked him what I was supposed to do with all the crap in my yard and he told me to do whatever I liked with it and then he shut the door in my face.

Well, I was never much of a golfer but I had a set of clubs in the garage. The three wood was just right for launching the dog crap. I took that three wood and I drove every one of those piles into the side of his house. Took about four hours for him to go outside and notice. He came over hopping mad."

"What did you tell him?" I asked.

"Rogue golfer. I told him I heard there was a rogue golfer in the neighborhood knocking dog crap against houses. And if he kept an eye out for the rogue dog I would be sure to watch out for the golfer. Never had crap in my yard again. And that is what I am getting at. Don't put up with any of it."

"But some of this goes without saying. Common sense."

"But people do it all the time. Of course I don't mind taking the restaurant table right by the bus station. It will probably be fine. Except it won't. What's more important in the long run? Getting to climb Machu Picchu once or spending twenty years not hearing shoes drop on your ceiling and not having somebody rattle ice outside your hotel door?"

I thought for a moment. I could hear Laura yelping after stubbing her toe for the umpteenth time on the bathroom threshold. If only I hadn't been taken in by the contractor. I needed to take her to Cuba when I came back. Somehow we were going to get in the back door and come back with some good stories for the neighbors. We'd fly in through Nicaragua or some such place. After the immunizations. And maybe with some of that prophylactic antibiotic that prevented Montezuma's revenge. I think that was how it worked. "Both," I finally said.

"Both?"

"Both. Otherwise you're just avoiding annoyances."

"It's more than annoyances. You think they're just annoyances. Pretty soon you tolerate more and that's when you elect a dictator. That's the downfall of great nations right there."

"Jerry," I said.

"Jerry what? Jerry, that's exaggerating? I'm eighty-seven years old and dead. I have a right to exaggerate. Except I'm not exaggerating. Every eastern bloc country after world war two went through this."

"Went through what? Bad apartments?"

"Among other things. No. They went though tolerating stranger and stranger things and adapting to an economy that made less and less sense. And then you get secret police."

I had to admit, the warmed over coffee pot was starting to look pretty good. At least better than Jerry's arguments. But it wouldn't be a bad title for a self-help book when I came back. If I came back. Unbucket: Prioritizing Life's Annoyances. Unbucket: The Truth that Climbed Machu Picchu. If I did both, managed to fill both lists, or empty one list and fill the other, or whatever the point was, I could become a motivational speaker when I came back. Come to think of it I could probably fill a house with the evangelists if I came up with a good vision about a tunnel and seeing a light. I would have to change it to that. They wouldn't want to hear about how I ran into some old guy on a vendetta.

"Maybe you're the reason I'm here," I blurted out to Jerry.

"Are you still going on about that sense of purpose thing? Why would I be the reason you're here?"

"So that I can write a great self-help book when I come back."

Jerry laughed. "Have you ever written anything other than an amortization table?"

"I must admit, I like your idea about the Unbucket. But I still think the big things are a better reason for me to come back. If there is someone, if God mulls these things over, I don't see how I would convince him of my worth by promising not to put up with restaurant tables near the bus station." And I could include the warning about throw rugs. Jerry might scoff at it, but I thought it could be helpful. Not only avoiding annoyances but making simple changes to save your life. That sounded catchy. Simple Changes to Save Your Life. If that wasn't a title I didn't know what was. There were already a hundred different books on simple changes to save money that just rehashed the same advice. They could have been subtitled "don't buy lattes" and it would have saved everyone time. I had never done anyone's taxes and found that lattes were the source of their financial woes. Usually it was the alimony, the real estate taxes, or the leased Jaguar that took the biggest bite out of their paycheck. And of course I had thought about writing that book, how to really save money, but instead I printed out some internet articles on not buying lattes and gave them to my clients who wanted a false sense of reassurance. But I would read a book about Simple Changes to Save Your Life. Wasn't that the first step in writing a best seller? Write about what you know?

The intern was still digging through the condiment bucket. "I swear I'm going to put mayo in my coffee on some night shift by mistake," said the intern.

"I've done that, Olson," True said. "I don't recommend it."

Olson grimaced. "Can't we put the bucket somewhere else? Can't we move it to the table away from the coffee pot." I craned my neck to read his name tag. Dr. Olson.

Putting the legos away. I had a box of those. And people kept giving me more legos. But I actually liked them as a kid. That didn't count. Model airplanes on the other hand, were the bane of my childhood. I never had the hand eye coordination to glue anything that small together or the patience then to read the instructions. But the bigger problem was that I wasn't very interested in airplanes, or tanks, or any of the minute specifications that were rendered in a one to seventy-two scale and all had to be separately glued. Yet as soon as another one showed up on a birthday I knew it was a matter of time before my father would expect to see the finished product, glue dried in clumps, wings askew, paint smudged onto the tiny plexiglass windows, and he would frown for a moment and then smile a little too broadly and give me a pep talk on how next time the glue wouldn't get away from me. And then he would want to go get another one and work on it with me. It wasn't that I didn't want to spend time with him, I would have loved to have spent time with him doing anything other than building a model airplane. But if I put it that way it always seemed to come across that I was ungrateful for the present. And then we were back to square one and I waxed poetic about how it was a great present and next time, yep, I wouldn't let the glue get away from me.

"I put the bucket in the cupboard once and somebody replaced it with this one and this one stayed," said True.

"What are you heating up?" Olson asked.

"Mashed potatoes," True said. The microwave beeped and she took out the Tupperware dish. She took a packet from the drawer and started sprinkling something over the top.

"What is that?" asked Olson.

"Do you have a lunch or are you going to stare at my food? Its funyuns."

"On potatoes?"

"Sure, it makes them crunchy."

Olson looked dejected. "This is a new low. I thought it was bad when I was hoarding the oyster crackers from the cafeteria to snack on something when they shut down after midnight."

"Suit yourself. But they're awesome on mashed potatoes," said True.

"Do you have any left in the bag?"

True handed the bag to Olson and he tapped a few crumbs into his palm. "More like None-yuns."

"Are you going to stare at my food while I eat?" asked True.

"No, no, of course not," Olson replied, looking back down at the condiment bucket again.

"Coffee cake," I said to Jerry. "You're right."

"About what?"

"About assumptions. I used to go visit my grandmother every other weekend with my parents when I was a kid. She always served coffee cake. I didn't like it. On the drive home my dad would complain to my mom that he didn't like it. And when Grandma would come over we would buy a coffee cake for her and we would all eat it. We were all out to breakfast one morning and about to order from the waitress. The breakfast specials came with a choice of sides: toast, corn muffin, or coffee cake. Grandma told her she wanted toast and then added 'I can't stand coffee cake.' My dad threw his napkin on the table and left the restaurant to go smoke in the parking lot. He had to come in and order late. We never had coffee cake after that."

Jerry looked at me quizzically.

"Not a lot of hardship when you were growing up, was there?"

"What's that supposed to mean?"

"Just that. But yes, that's how it starts. Good thing it didn't progress to garden gnomes. Those things give me the creeps with their beady little eyes."

Olson was leaning over True's food again.

"Don't you have a conference that feeds you?" True asked.

"If you call it food," he replied.

There was a marker on the shelf that ran the length of the wall and Jerry deftly picked it up and set down the envelope. I watched as he wrote "Confidential, destroy if found."

"What if they destroy it?"

"What if they recycle it instead because it's boring? They won't destroy it. We need to capture their interest."

"You could squirt some mayonnaise in their coffee," I suggested.

"Don't knock it. Bad food is bonding. My wife and I met in the Philippines in the war. Millie was deployed there as a dietician. They served something called 'regional stew' in the chow hall. I never could find out if it was referring to a geographic region of the country or an anatomic region of the animal. She never could either, but we ate a lot of mystery meat together before the war was over. If these two get desperate enough to put mayo in the coffee, they'll be married by next June."

Jerry went back to work on the envelope, underlining 'destroy.'

Then with seemingly practiced aim, he threw the marker into the metal trash can under the coffee station. The loud clang was his cover. He slid the envelope toward True and Intern Olson, knocking the left over donut pieces to the floor as it went past.

"Was that here when we sat down?" the intern asked.

"How would I know," True said.

"Are those wasabi peas?" asked Olson. He reached past the envelope and picked up a packet of little green things covered in dust.

"Those are really old wasabi peas," said True.

"I thought everything got eaten in the ER. How long have these been there?"

"At least four years. Do you want them? We'll put your name on the bulletin board with a star if you actually eat them. It's become sort of a game to see if anyone will."

Olson looked down at the package. "The package is open so someone did."

"Opened and then let them sit. They are very, very stale."

Olson looked thoughtful for a moment. "Do you mind if I borrow these?"

"Suit yourself," said True.

"Trauma, level one, room four. Trauma, level one, room four."

"Do not eat this while I'm in the trauma," True said, pointing a finger at Olson.

"While you're in the trauma? I'm going to be in there too."

"You're going to be watching from a safe distance is more like it."

They jumped up and left the break room, neither taking the envelope.

Jerry looked crestfallen.

I picked up the envelope. "If they see it again, they'll definitely look at it. Déjà vu and all. Come on, we'll have another chance."

Jerry and I followed them. There was a gurney parked in the hallway under a sign that said "2C" and two teenage boys sat side by side on it. One had an icepack on his knee and the other had an icepack pressed to his nose. I did a double-take. It was the kids from the train. Before I could say anything, the first kid shouted at True. "Hey, Nurse. Why are we parked in the hallway?"

"Because the ER is busy today. This is an overflow bed."

"Are you both here to be seen?" asked Olson.

"Nah," said the second kid. "I know my nose is probably broke. Whatever, right? I'm just here with my friend. He hurt his leg."

"How long until I see the doctor? My leg is killing me," said the first kid.

Olson sniffed and looked at True. "What is that smell?" he asked.

"Its teen spirit," True said to Olson in reply. "You hurled on your buddy?" asked True to the first kid.

"What? No way. Some dude threw up on my shoe. It wasn't me."

"Wow," said True. "A drive by vomiting. I'm sure it wasn't you."

"Seriously, it wasn't. How long until I see the doctor?" asked the first kid again.

True sighed. "Could be a while. What happened to you anyways?"

"You don't want to know. Man, these three dudes on the train," the first kid began.

"Three big dudes," added the second kid.

"Three big dudes. They came out of nowhere."

"They jumped us," added the second kid.

"Le t me take a wild guess," said True. "What were you doing when this all went down?"

"We were minding our own business!" they said together.

"We'll get a doctor over to you right away," said True, as she rolled her eyes. "Come on Olson."

"How did you know they were minding their own business?" asked Olson.

"Because that's the most dangerous occupation in the city. Usually people mind their own business outside a liquor store or on their way home from church. And it's always at least two dudes. But sometimes it's that bitch or my cousin," explained True.

"Your cousin?" asked Olson.

True sighed. "As in question: who shot you? Answer: my cousin. Or question: who beat you up? Answer: two dudes that came out of nowhere. Or question: who stabbed you? Answer: that bitch. Come on, Olson. We have a trauma."

"But you told those guys you were going to get a doctor right away," Olson stammered.

True muttered something and kept walking toward room 4.

Jerry noticed me staring nervously at the two kids on the cart. I was about to explain the whole fight on the train when he shrugged. "Two punks like that? If they gave me any crap I would just kick one in the kneecap and smash the other one in the nose. Looks like someone beat me to it."

Chapter 9

Loud voices came from room seventeen. "Just hold still, sir. You need this medication."

"I need to share my soul with the world. I can show you. I can take a gun, just get me a gun, I can take you all out with me. Going higher, higher to the sky and the planets are alive, alive, alive!" The words came as fast as the young man could spit them.

Olson turned to True. "Is that the trauma?"

True shook her head. "That's the manic guy that came in a couple hours ago. The social worker was trying to talk him down enough so he wouldn't need to get restrained. She got him to take some ativan pills but you can see how well that worked. The cops have him under an emergency

Chapter to get him a mental health bed. They've been here all night waiting for one to open up because they were here when I left my last shift. Milking the overtime, I swear. No, our guy is in room four."

Room four was a hive of activity. A man wheeled in on a stretcher with a mountain of gauze taped to his chest. There was the barest suggestion of a metal object sticking out of his chest.

"Oh my God, Jerry, I think he was stabbed," I said.

"He probably deserved it. Keep an eye on those two so we can feed them the chart."

"He probably deserved it? What kind of a thing is that to say? You don't even know him. Somebody stabbed this guy," I said.

Dr. Maglio was leaning against the wall assessing the patient from a distance. The man was yelling obscenities at everyone within a mile radius so Jerry might have been right but I wasn't going to admit it.

"Who are you?" Maglio asked the young woman writing down notes as the paramedics gave report.

"I'm True's nursing student. I'm the trauma recorder but this is my first time."

"Med prompt, paging Dr. Time. There is no one by that name. Med Prompt" came a tinny voice from the intern's scrub pocket.

"And first time with one of those voice-activated time savers in your pocket too? Can you turn that thing off for the trauma?" snapped Maglio.

"Med Prompt. Paging Dr. El Ramaa. Med Prompt."

"I didn't push any buttons," said the nurse intern in alarm.

"Just turn it off."

"But I'm not supposed to."

"Do you want to talk to Dr. El Ramaa when he calls back in five minutes and explain why a nurse intern is paging him? He's a neurosurgeon with an attitude."

"No I don't. I'm turning it off, I'm turning it off," she said.

"Med Prompt. Connecting. Med Prompt," it beeped as the nurse intern pushed the middle button frantically.

"Give me that," said Maglio. He grabbed the MedPrompt out of her hand, expertly popped out the battery from the back and handed it back. "Now when Dr. El Ramaa calls back it will get bounced to the main ER number, the secretaries will overhead it, no one will pay attention, he'll still be a pissed off neurosurgeon but he won't be pissed at you. See how easy that was?"

"Wow, thanks, Dr. Maglio," she said.

"By the way True, I haven't seen you spending much time with your student today," said Maglio. "Did you set her up with this great technology?"

True rolled her eyes. "She's not my student; Donna pawned her off. Be nice to her. Why don't you pay attention to your patient?"

Maglio turned back to the nurse intern. "True's-nursing student, make a note that the patient has an intact airway."

"But you haven't examined him yet."

"Did you hear what he just called me? If he can yell that from across the room, he has an airway, believe me. Vocabulary and airway are linked, got that Olson? Hey guys," Maglio stopped the paramedic as they were about to leave.

"Doc?"

"Just what is the object that you have so carefully stabilized in gauze?"

The one medic grinned and began to unwrap their masterpiece. As the layers fell away, one could see a metal handle and a long metal rod protruding from the patient's chest. At the base, held in place by several tines, was a large, pink, fleshy strip of some material.

"Oh my god, is that his pectoralis muscle?" This time the question came from Intern Olson and True tried to suppress her laughter with snorting into her elbow.

"Dr. Olson. Why don't you examine the patient more closely. It would be remarkable if the pectoralis muscle managed to get turned inside out and landed on top of the patient's skin."

The intern warily approached the other man who was momentarily quiet, perhaps stunned at the realization that he indeed had some sort of serving fork sticking out of his chest. In fact he was staring down at his chest with eyes the size of dinner plates.

"I don't know what it is," the intern said. "It looks like a piece of muscle."

"Correct," said Maglio. "But not his muscle." He turned back toward the paramedics. "Did you really have to leave the Sunday ham on the end of the fork?"

"Impaled objects. That's what we do. Stabilize the object."

"That's ham?" the nursing student asked incredulously.

"If you look closely, you'll note that it is honey-baked ham," said Maglio.

True rolled her eyes in the general direction of Maglio. "You can really tell that from across the room?"

"I didn't get a break for lunch today. Can I help it if I'm hungry?"

The patient spat another string of expletives directed toward everyone in the room.

"True, how do I chart this in the trauma paperwork? Should I call it ham or maybe lunchmeat, but if they were having a Sunday dinner it wasn't just lunch meat," mused the student.

"Dr. Olson. Please pull the fork out of the patient. You can do whatever you like with the dinner leftovers. He needs a two view chest to prove that this is the superficial wound that I know it to be and then you can stitch him closed."

"I'm just putting down unknown dinner meat," the nursing student announced.

"Hey man, I want the fork back," the patient said to Olson.

"You what?"

"You heard me, Doogie Howser. I want the fork back. It's a serving set from my mother. It's genuine silver, man. Bonafide. My damn cousin better not have bent it or he'll be wearing it next."

Olson looked like he'd won a spelling bee. "Was it really your cousin?" he asked the man.

"Of course it was my damn cousin. What did I just say?"

"True, you were so right!" Olson exclaimed.

"Olson, while you're waiting for that x-ray, why don't you help me push room six up to the unit?" said True, rolling her eyes.

"Room six?"

"The emphysema guy we put on the vent. I think you missed it, you were in the room with the other cardiac arrest earlier. Anyways, he's been waiting for a bed in the ICU for four hours."

"I can go right now," Olson said, a little too quickly, as he backed away from the patient.

"Oh no you don't. The ventilator is breathing for the other guy. You got a fork to pull," said Maglio.

Olson grimaced and inched toward the angry punctured man. "Do I literally just pull it out?"

"No intern, you use the special ham fork removal device that we keep in room 4 for these special occasions. Just. Pull. It. Out."

Olson did not look convinced. "It's the chest cavity. There's a lot of stuff in there."

Maglio was frowning at him. "Stuff?"

"Heart. Lungs," offered Olson, "And some really big blood vessels. Don't you think we need an x-ray first to make sure it doesn't go in that deep?"

"Oh for goodness sake." True reached in front of Olson and pulled out the fork. The patient yelped and brought his right arm up to cover the small punctures left behind. The injury looked a lot less dramatic with the fork gone. "You can have this back when the police are done with it. It's evidence," she said to the patient.

The patient began describing just what he wasn't going to do to his cousin and his cousin's mother. I was waiting for one of the ER staff to tell him something about keeping it in the family but they seemed so used to such tirades that they were no longer listening. Maglio was texting on his cell phone and the nurse intern was checking off boxes on her paperwork.

"Sorry Maglio. I have to pee and if I don't get the vent patient upstairs first I'm going to hear it from the ICU manager."

"Fork you, bitch," shouted the patient.

This caught Maglio's attention. "Listen Ham Fork, that was uncalled for. From everything you just said, it sounds like you keep the forking in your family so how about we keep it that way?"

The intern and True left Ham Fork yelling behind them and headed to room six.

The secretary's voice came through over the din. "I know it's you. You called and hung up on me earlier today. We haven't found them and at this point I don't think we will. Yes, we looked in the x-ray department. You can file a complaint. I would be happy to give you that number."

True called across the ER. "Is that the nipple ring guy?"

The secretary rolled her eyes. The handset was back in the cradle. "He hung up on me again."

"Wait," said Olson. "Did you say nipple ring guy?"

"Yep, he keeps calling. He took them off for x-ray and now they're missing," said True.

"I would be too embarrassed to call about something like that."

"You wouldn't if it was your good pair," dead panned True.

"Ow," said Olson. "Do you see a lot of that?"

"More and more. It's kind of a problem for scans. X-ray it will just show up on the film but for scans they cause a bunch of static so you can't see whole sections of the patient. They all attach differently. We really should get a tool box for the ER and be done with it."

"And it's a guy that keeps calling?" Olson asked.

"Are you still stuck on that? Yes, it's a guy."

"Have you ever seen a pierced, you know," Olson began.

"I've seen a pierced everything. I love talking to the girls about it. I'm not going there, believe me, my earrings are enough, but we're the after-hours gynecology clinic for the girls and it's a crazy life."

"The girls?" asked Olson.

"The working girls. Geez Olson. Are you going to make it through your month here? I don't want you to have a seizure the first time you go do an STD check on a hooker with a pierced hoohah," said True.

Olson was pale. He seemed like a good kid. At least he seemed to have a sense of decorum and it didn't include pierced genitalia.

"Now is our chance. We can put the file right on the guy's bed," said Jerry.

"What?" I asked.

"Get your mind out of the gutter so mine can go floating by. We can put the file right here."

"What if he's stuck? What if he's like us and he's wandering around the hospital somewhere?" I asked.

"Haven't seen anybody other than you. Apparently this sort of thing doesn't happen very often. Haven't ever seen a pierced hoohah either, come to think of it. I would like to wrap up this project and have a little free time around this place."

"This entire experience is just creepy," I blurted out.

"Are you going to start complaining again? Come on. If we don't ride up in the elevator we won't know how to find this guy. Besides he doesn't sound that dead. I was on a ventilator twice and came back each time."

Alvarez walked up to True and Olson as they were about to leave. "True, where's your intern?"

"My what?"

"Your nurse intern. Her husband's here and says he has to pick something up from her."

"From her? She's in room 4. I'll get her." She looked pointedly at Olson. "Watch this guy. If anything alarms for more than five seconds come get me."

True stuck her head around the curtain. "Becky? Betty?"

"It's Angie."

"Right, sorry Angie. Your husband is here. He said he needs to pick something up. This better not be a conjugal visit because we don't allow those."

"A what visit?" asked the nurse intern.

"Joking. Never mind," said True. "What is he here to pick up anyways?"

"Milk. I'm pumping. We have a ten month old."

"You're pumping?" asked True incredulously. "Where?"

"In the break room."

"In the break room? But the break room is, it's not, I mean, why?"

"It's nasty? Yes, it is. But it works. Besides after this month I'm precepting on labor and delivery and they have a real pumping room."

"But where do you put it?" True looked around wide-eyed.

"In the fridge."

True raised an eyebrow.

"In the fridge in a sealed bottle inside a bag with my name on it. I know people take food out of there. I don't think anybody will take this," the nurse intern said, laughing.

"Angie, I am so sorry. I can't believe you didn't mention this before. Look, if you need time to go do what you need to do, just let me know. Maybe you can pump somewhere more private."

"True, it's OK. I didn't want to really talk about it before. I didn't want to advertise it to the department when I'm new here. Do you want to see little Zoey's picture?"

True smiled. "I do. When I'm back from the unit with the vent guy. That's a sweet name."

True was busy attaching the monitor leads to the portable monitor and detaching everything else from the wall. The nurse intern passed by them carrying a brown paper bag as she walked out to the waiting room. True looked up as she pushed the exit button and the doors by the mural swung open.

"Olson, is she carrying a Genius Bagels bag?" True asked.

Olson was flustered. "What? I didn't notice. I was getting the patient ready."

True rolled her eyes at him. "I hope not."

"You hope I'm not getting him ready?"

"I hope I don't have to kill Maglio. Never mind." She glanced back toward Maglio and then looked at the man on the ventilator. "We need to go upstairs."

"Security, STAT, Security, STAT, Waiting Room, Security, STAT, Waiting Room." The tinny robotic voice blared out of an overhead speaker along with a flashing blue light and a bone-jarring buzzer that sounded every five seconds. I watched as two nurses got up and began closing patients' doors and pulling curtains.

The nurse intern was back and she looked more excited now than apprehensive. "Are we getting another trauma?" she asked True.

"No, we'd have it by now if we were. It's probably just another fight in the waiting room," said True.

"Seriously?"

"Seriously. We lock the doors so it won't spill over into here."

The director looked over her glasses at the nurse intern. "Its usually about who's been waiting the longest. The whole concept of triage is great for academic reading but it doesn't fly with half-assed patient satisfaction surveys. Cut finger, waited five minutes, got three stitches and went home, happy patient. Waited four hours because we were saving someone's life, maybe your neighbor's life? Unhappy patient. Because we can't go announce to the waiting room that somebody is having a heart attack and we're just a little busy and need all hands on deck. Violates confidentiality."

The nurse intern frowned. "But it's the ER. Don't people know what happens here?"

"The ambulances come in through the garage so the waiting room never sees it. The only time they get it is when somebody staggers in blue, collapses, and we start CPR in the waiting room," the director said.

"Or that time I delivered a baby in the chair," True chimed in.

"You delivered a baby by yourself?" the nurse intern gasped.

"She caught the baby. The mom delivered it," the director said.

"Thank you for the clarification. Do you want to explain the birds and bees too?" True rolled her eyes.

"I seem to recall it took you a minute or two to figure out that she was actually having a baby," the director replied.

"Hey, you weren't there. You were back in the department dealing with the two gunshots that day."

"Was that the day the two guys shot each other? I mean, I know we get that a lot, but I mean those two guys that shot each other and then got dropped off by the same car," the director said.

"No it was the day that other guy shot his finger tip off."

"Oh that guy. That guy that had the whole one in a million story for the cops."

"That he was minding his own business?"

"Right. And he was right handed and his left index finger was missing a tip, and there were powder burns on his pants but he couldn't possibly have been cleaning his gun," said the director.

"Why would it matter that he was cleaning his gun?" Olson asked. "Was he just embarrassed?"

"I'm sure he was embarrassed but he was on parole from something and he wasn't supposed to have a gun. That was the bigger problem. That's why it takes cops such a long time to sort this stuff out because its either their gun or the victim was doing something else illegal when they got victimized so the stories get very creative. Anyways True, that was the guy. I remember him. Fat and not that bright. I kept telling him to keep his hand elevated and every time I checked on him he was dangling his hand at his side and it would start dripping again. He was kind of drunk too," the director trailed off, shaking her head.

"I bet you didn't expect to see a baby crowning in the waiting room," the nurse intern said to True.

"I didn't even see that. The kid was halfway out before I saw anything. But the mom was screaming and she didn't speak a lot of English so at first I didn't know what the problem was."

"You really delivered the baby by yourself," the nurse intern asked.

"That was the easy part. The hard part was getting the mom's pants off without her falling out of the chair. It was baby number four and he wasn't waiting," True laughed.

"Didn't you get a standing ovation that day?" the director asked.

"That was OK. The best part was that I was just finishing up my triage booth hour and after that I went into the department and half the people in the waiting room were my patients for the next couple of hours. Everyone was sweet as apple pie. I got high fives and everything. They said it was like TV."

"You think the new group will get approval for the educational TV in the waiting room?" the director asked.

"Of course they will," True said. She pointed to the mural. "They got that, didn't they?"

"For the record, if they actually asked for that as a priority then I have even more fear for the future of this place. Short of a TV, I volunteered a couple of times to stage a big code and run it through the waiting room. You know, lay on a gurney, tape some IVs and ventilator equipment on and have the staff do a few laps shouting STAT."

"You can dress me up like a pregnant lady and I can lie there and yell that I need to push," True offered.

"Seriously, we're too discreet saving lives behind the curtain. We need to remind people why we're here."

"Now you're talking like someone who is thinking about staying on with the new group," True said.

The director sighed. "No, I'm not. Definitely not. But it's a problem in nine out of ten ERs. Quote me. The grass is just a little bit greener at St. Pat's but don't worry, I'll find plenty to gripe about there too." She grinned. "Excuse me." I watched as she got up in response to a grey-haired man waving at her from room seventeen.

Jerry and I kept an eye on True and the intern but we walked after the director.

Jerry shook his head. "That's what's wrong with society today."

"What's wrong," I asked.

"No sense of community."

"No sense of community? Aren't you the same guy who chased your neighbors off your porch with a shotgun and took potshots at your other neighbor's house with a golf club?"

"That's different. And it wasn't loaded, by the way, it was just to make a point. And I took potshots with dog crap. The golf club was only the delivery device."

The director was talking with a man wringing his hands. A tearful woman stood next to him with an arm around his shoulder.

"Is he going to ever be normal again? I don't know where to begin. Do we need to sell his house in Indiana? Do I need to call his job and tell them he isn't coming back? I'm sorry to be taking up all your time, I can tell its busy here today but I just don't know where to begin. He's never been like this before. He was a normal kid. A completely normal kid."

The director put her hand on his arm. "That's a bit premature. Don't call his job yet, OK? I'm not pretending this is good news but if this is a manic episode he may very well be able to live with it once he settles down. Right now we can't really talk to him he's so amped up. You said so yourself."

"I know, I know," the man's father shook his head. "But you had to sedate him. You saw how he grabbed his mother's arm like that. It was like he didn't even know who we were."

"I don't want to be afraid of my son," said the woman.

"He didn't know who you were. Not really," said the director.

"You're sure his cat scan is normal? No brain tumor?" the father asked.

"It was normal. That's the other reason I sedated him so much. I wanted to make sure he would be still for the scan."

"That's good then, right? Not that I wish it was a tumor, but…" he trailed off and stared at the ground.

"But if it was a tumor then it could be removed and he would be OK? I know what you mean. This isn't something that we can remove. But he hasn't slept in five days. He's going to get some rest. He's going to get some medication and then the psychiatrist can talk to him and get a better idea of what's going on. Plenty of people live with this and lead normal lives."

"Like who?" asked the father.

The director paused. Jerry and I both leaned in to hear the answer.

"I hope she doesn't say Vincent Van Gogh," Jerry said.

"Winston Churchill," the director said.

"You're not serious," the father said.

"I am," she said. "He had more issues with depression than manic episodes but he called depression a little black dog that followed him around. To say that he learned to deal with it would be an understatement." She smiled.

"Thanks, doc," said the father.

Chapter 10

Jerry and I followed True and Olson as they pushed the patient down the hallway.

"True, why didn't you go to medical school? You're way smarter than me," said Olson.

"Please. You're just saying that to get in my pants."

"I tried that. You said I was too young anyways."

"No, I said I have children and I don't date children. If I say you're too young then that makes me too old. Which I'm not. It's a mental age. But why I didn't go to medical school, hmm. That's a big question. If I try to explain it you'll think I'm blaming my shortcomings on my mother."

"I don't mind. I blame my going to medical school on my mother and I think it might have been the worst thing I could have done."

"Intern year is the worst thing. There's a difference. I've seen enough interns come and go. You'll be fine. Your parents encouraged you?"

"You could say that," Olson replied.

"My mother and father were divorced. My mother was a CNA in a nursing home and hated her job but told me I should go become a CNA too because of the job security," said True.

"Maybe she was just looking out for you."

"Maybe she wanted me to share in her misery loves company way of life."

"Maybe she couldn't see the big picture," offered Olson.

"Actually she had a very big picture. And but for her children she would have become a nun. That was her big picture. And she reminded us of this on a regular basis. She stood up her date with God in order to slum and have kids."

"Wow," said Olson.

"She was a piece of work. She sent me a long letter when I turned forty, the same year my idiot ex moved out. She had a falling out with a nun when she was in school. She was in a play and had on red woolen long underwear to play the part of the devil. Well, after the play, it was cold out, she had to walk home in the snow, something like that, she forgot to take off the red long underwear and turn it in with the rest of the costumes. Not a big deal, right? Apparently, when she went to school the next day, Sister Beneficence, or whatever she called herself, read her the riot act about how she had stolen from the school and what a lousy kid she was."

They turned the corner headed toward the elevator and Olson kicked at one of the wheels that was stuck. "My estimation of the Catholic church just went a little bit lower."

I shifted to Jerry's left so that I could pass by the next hand washing station and test it. If he saw me try the motion detector this time, he didn't say anything. I never slept well in hotels. My last business trip, I'd stayed up and watched one of those ghost hunter shows where they test houses with thermal cameras and such. There was something about ectoplasm or was it protoplasm, I thought, good grief. As if bad hotel television was going to explain my situation. I wasn't a ghost. It was just a matter of time before everything would be normal again. I reached into the paper towel dispenser, pulled out a towel, crumpled it, and threw it at Jerry.

Olson watched it sail past, frowned, and looked up toward the vent in the ceiling.

"No kidding. But she was about ten at the time," True continued. "Don't you think that would be old enough to stand up and say that the teacher was wrong, or at least to think it? According to the letter, this sent my mother into some tailspin where she didn't feel she could hack it as a nun so she got married instead."

"Wow, did she send a copy to your dad as well? Did he know he was the consolation prize for the bride of Christ?"

"I never asked him. I'm sure it factored into their divorce. Anyway, she goes on and on in the letter about how due to her great sacrifice, I exist and so do my four kids and she can take credit for that."

"That is about the most over the top Catholic guilt trip I think I have heard of."

"Glad you think so. You know, getting it at forty, I had more of a laugh over it then anything else. But I think that attitude must have permeated my childhood. Anyways, I wasn't going to get any scholarship to higher education and mom wasn't going to help. So life happened. When it came time to decide what do to with the rest of my life, I just wanted to be a better mom to my kids and career came second. Now that I am here," she gestured at the patient stretched out in the bed, monitors beeping, ventilator sighing in and out, "Doing this all day, not sure if I'm getting ahead or if this guy is, I'm not so sure."

"That's why I'm not sure going into medicine was the right thing for me."

"Why?"

"All the rearranging of deck chairs on the Titanic that we do, all the chronic management of stuff that we can't cure."

Jerry perked up. "He's not such an idiot!" he said earnestly.

"Well, that's encouraging," I replied.

"It's true though," he said, pointing down at the patient in the gurney. "This guy would be better off with a pack of smokes and a shot of whiskey than all this nonsense. Go out with a bang," said Jerry. He looked up and down the hall as if he might find a vending machine to supply the contraband.

"You mean make the oxygen tubing explode?"

"No, I mean he'd be better off enjoying a few vices in peace. Then bar the door and don't let the paramedics in the house. But exploding the oxygen tubing; that would be dramatic. Maybe we can do that in front of the board of directors." Jerry fell silent, no doubt plotting just how to manage that.

True and Olson muscled the bed into the elevator and we stepped on as well. The door squeaked to a close and True and Olson were pressed flat against the wall. I realized that Jerry and I were actually partially in the wall, which he seemed to find amusing. I didn't like it at all. It was bad enough being in an unfamiliar place with Jerry for company. If I started walking through walls I would have no sense of direction.

Jerry elbowed me in the ribs. "Goes right through you, see?"

"Don't do that," I said.

"Why?"

"I told you before. It gives me the creeps. I don't like the idea of walking through walls." I thought about the CEO's office door again. The polished wood. It reminded me of a coffin lid, I suddenly realized. Jerry could think whatever he wanted about destiny. I had to get out of this situation.

"I think it's interesting. Once in a lifetime experience. Besides, you keep treating the paper towel dispenser like the magic eight ball of your mortality and while it doesn't give me the creeps, I do find it annoying."

"I'm just using it as a barometer. It's something consistent I can check. They all have the same sensors. Didn't you ever take physics? I wasn't very good at it but the laws were consistent. If the sensor is infra-red then I should be able to set it off." I said. "And anyways, I'm going to save the experience of walking through stuff for when I'm really dead."

"So the next office we have to get into, I'll waltz through the wall and you'll be stuck outside trying to pick the lock?"

"Jerry, I don't even know how to pick locks. My only point it I don't want to be reminded of my predicament and you putting an arm through my ribs tends to remind me."

"You can't pick locks?" He was incredulous.

"No, I can't pick locks. Let me guess, this is some manly skill I was supposed to pick up along the way?"

"I learned it from my shop teacher. But you probably took home economics. If you're going to take the high and mighty 'when I'm really dead' attitude as if this is just a brief visit to go slumming with an old guy, at least you should know how to pick locks."

"Fine, Jerry," I said. "Obviously you feel a need to teach me. Why exactly did your shop teacher teach you this criminal skill?"

"Criminal? What are you, a moron? Haven't you ever been locked out of your house or your car?"

"Of course I have."

"So what did you do?"

"I called triple A the first time and I walked to a neighbor's house the second time and called a locksmith out of the yellow pages."

Jerry groaned. "Very resourceful. Good thing you weren't headed west in a covered wagon. Triple A. You're probably one of those types with a GPS thing in your car too. Drive your car into a pond because the GPS told you to. You can make a lock picking tool out of the spoon on the Swiss army knife."

"The Swiss army knife doesn't come with a spoon."

"The good one does. The big one. Not the little trinket one you get in a cereal box."

I was about to tell Jerry that I was pretty sure you couldn't get a knife in a cereal box when the elevator lurched. I didn't want to get stuck in the elevator with the guy on the ventilator and Jerry. And if they knew, I'm sure True and Olson wouldn't have wanted to be stuck in there with me.

"It's not the chronic management stuff that bugs me," said True.

"No?" said Olson.

"No. How can I put this? I think it's the paperwork."

"Every job has paperwork."

"I don't mean just doing paperwork. It's the way the paperwork just checks everything off and pretends you have it covered. Here, fill out the septic shock packet, here, fill out the level one trauma packet. Breathing? Check. Hemorrhaging? Check. Time of death? Check. Called the chaplain? Check. Met with family? Check. Done deal. Great patient care. It's a little bit too automatic."

Olson nodded. "I know what you mean."

"It's all packaged. That's what it is. I hate the fact that we have an information packet that we actually give families when someone dies. I mean, I know they need it and it answers a lot of questions and all that and maybe they'll read it later and call the crisis number or something. But I feel like a movie usher handing out the program. Here, we've thought of everything. Did your loved one just die? Have this pamphlet, it will answer all your questions. Next."

"But you have to give them something!" Olson sounded distressed.

"I know, I know. And I don't have time to run home in the middle of my shift and make chicken soup for them, OK? I know. But I want to tell them, here is this stupid pamphlet with a bunch of feel good stuff that will probably not be worth a damn but we have to give you something according to our protocol but I am so sorry because there is no pamphlet that will make any of this better."

"But you could say that," Olson said. "You could say something like that maybe leaving out the stupid and the damn."

True smiled. "You know who does that? Maglio. Maglio is such a pain in the ass but he is really good with families. He has a great way of saying just that and yes, he leaves out the stupid and the damn. You'd be amazed. Behind the curtain with the families, he's really kind. I wish I could put it as well as he does."

"But the nurses don't have to give the announcement to the families do they?"

True laughed harshly. "No, Olson. We don't. The docs give the news. And then after a few minutes, the docs leave and the nurse is left with the family for the next three hours. And it's hours because of course more family has to arrive and they need to hear the story too. And then the shock hits and there's crying and screaming and sometimes the family starts throwing chairs. I've had that happen before more than once. The chair throwing thing. And then I run out of things to say and I give them a pamphlet."

"Where do they set the pamphlet if they threw the chair?" Olson asked.

'What?"

"Where do they put it if they threw the chair?"

True laughed again. "Olson, you're such an ass."

They both looked down at their patient whose chest was rising and falling in rhythm as the ventilator sighed. The cardiac monitor traced a jagged green line while the elevator lurched upward.

"I wish we could be like that," True said.

"Like what?"

"Like the monitor. Like a machine. Just clock in and clock out. Like an MRI machine or something. Give people what they need without having to feel."

"But that's not what they need," said Olson.

"I know, I know," said True. "I don't really think that. I just feel that way sometimes. It would make my job easier."

They watched the monitor again.

The elevator stopped and the doors opened to a crowd of white coats who looked in at the ventilator patient. They frowned as the doors closed.

"True?" asked Olson.

"What?"

"How did you get your name? I mean, why aren't you named after a saint?"

"It's short for Prudence."

"You're kidding."

"You asked."

"Then why isn't it Prudie or Pru?"

"Would you want to be named Prudie or Pru?"

Olson thought for a moment. "Good point. True is a great name."

True smiled. "I sort of picked it out myself in high school and it stuck."

"That's amazing. That is so original," gushed Olson.

"Not really. It's kind of adolescent. But I got into a few fights over it when other kids kept calling me a prude. I've got a couple of tattoos from the same time in my life that weren't the best idea. But it's my name."

"Am I really too young for you?"

"Oh for Pete's sake," she said, blushing.

"You're meeting me at a very awkward point in my life. I have to wear this short white coat. I'm too tired to bother putting my contacts in and honestly even showering and getting a haircut take a backseat to sleep when I get the chance. I look like absolute crap every day. I'm my least funny, least nice, least smart, most stressed. It can only improve after this year."

"At which point you will get the long white coat and the air of confidence to put the moves on every nursing student between here and Holy Tony's and you'll turn into another asshole," said True.

"Wow. Bitter."

"The last one didn't end well."

"Was it with a doc?"

"No way."

"Who was it with?"

"A guy," True said. "A guy I was with after the ex moved out."

"What ended it?"

"Nothing ever ends it, you know. It's never anything as dramatic as walking in on someone else in the bed. It just switches off with me. One final gripe and then I'm done. With him it was about peeing in the shower."

"You left him because he peed in the shower? That seems like an overreaction."

"No Olson. I left him because he complained about me peeing in the shower."

"OK, that's gross. I mean, maybe I do that once in a while. But like, as a habit? I would think you could have worked it out."

"It was the principle. It was the realization that he was never going to understand me."

"Is this a habit that is so important to you? I could probably deal with it if it was."

True sighed in exasperation. "It's not my habit. It had been a long week. I had worked three double shifts, had a parent-teacher meeting with nuns about my youngest kid again, and finally had a chance to have a beer and relax on the couch. And it came up in conversation. It came up along the lines of being so tired I could sleep standing up in the shower too. And I meant for it to be ha,ha funny and instead he headed upstairs with windex and a scouring pad."

"Did you tell him you were through that night?"

"Nah. It had been brewing for a while anyway. I think he was sublimating cleaning for something else. There is a point where maybe you don't do it on the floor the moment you get in the house but you also shouldn't get in the house and head right to the grout brush and go to town."

"Is that a metaphor for something that I should know?"

"No. Scrubbing grout is just scrubbing grout."

"Oh, too bad. I thought it might be a new euphemism. Like, hey, want to scrub grout with me? Do me like grout. Grout me. Something like that. So where is he now?"

"Hooked up with a dude."

"What?!"

"Kidding," True said.

"That would have been awesome though."

"It would only have been awesome if it was an ugly dude."

"But wouldn't you have felt bad then? If he left you for someone worse looking?"

"You know, Olson, if I had no self esteem I would take that to mean I was bad looking but they were worse," True said.

"Oh shoot. No, I didn't mean it that way," Olson said, his eyes wide with fear.

"Does my butt look big in these scrubs? Tell me the truth and I'll cry," laughed True.

Olson looked panicked and Jerry was laughing so hard it was hard to hear over him.

"It doesn't look big," Olson stammered.

"Don't lie, now I'll cry anyway."

"Are you messing with me?" Olson asked.

"Do you have to ask?"

"I hate it when girls do that."

"Me too," said True. "And guys do it too, more often than you think. Anyway, I would have gotten a kick out of Mr. Fastidious coming out of the closet but not being able to score with a hot guy.

But honestly, I have no idea where he is now or what he's doing. This is a big enough city. It's a catch 22. Dating from work is never a good idea. And dating medical is never a good idea. And I think I attract people with a mommy-complex. No offense. But if I get invited to one more apartment with inflatable furniture by some guy with Charlie Brown sweaters I think I will just give up on the whole scene. But this last guy was such a germaphobe. I should have known ahead of time it wasn't going to work. He was paranoid I was going to bring some incurable disease home from work and give it to him. Didn't worry about me getting it mind you. Worried about me giving it to him."

"Like your syphilis?"

"Right. Screw you, Olson. Go grout yourself. He was a selfish guy though. He never understood the concept of a night shift either. He'd call from the office at 10 am to make plans right when I was hitting REM. Anyway, we almost broke up earlier when I made a joke about hepatitis bear."

"Hepatitis what?"

"Hepatitis bear. Jake had this bear that a friend of mine gave him when he was a baby. I thought it was just made out of alpaca wool. It was really fuzzy and had this really long fur. Very cute. He brought it to me when he was about three years old and told me I needed to fix Teddy because he had a rip. No big deal, right? When you're a mom you stitch up stuffed animals all the time. When I took a look at the bear though, I realized that it was made out of alpaca hide. This was not going to stitch up well with an ordinary sewing kit."

Olson interrupted. "I know, sutures, right?"

"Exactly. I brought home some size four nylon with the big curved needle and some alligator forceps and got to work. The fur was so fluffy though that it was really hard to see the suture or find the needle and I stuck myself a couple of times. Germaphobe walks in while I'm in the middle of this and was just horrified that I was doing this procedure on a stuffed animal."

"What's the big deal?"

"He told me later that it was because he was afraid of needles. I don't think that was it. Anyways, I had just poked my finger and it was bleeding a little bit and I was cursing at the bear. He asked me what the heck I was doing and I told him at least the bear didn't have hepatitis."

Olson laughed. "And he didn't think that was funny?"

"Not even a little bit. But I finished suturing the bear. That's the problem though. You do this long enough you get a little warped. Normal people don't think certain things are funny. Then me, I make jokes about hepatitis to the kindergarten teacher the following year and get blacklisted from the bake sale and wonder why."

"Did that really happen?"

"Olson, it's a metaphor. Besides, bake sales are a pain. I don't do them. If the school wants extra money out of me I would rather just give them ten bucks then spend an hour making snickerdoodles."

"You don't bake?" Olson asked wistfully.

"Only when I have to. And stop looking at me like that. I already told you I don't date children."

"You hardly know me."

"Believe me, Olson. You don't need my chaos. You need one of those condos with the really mod furniture and a maid. And if you still have the inflatable furniture you need to ditch it so you have a chance at getting laid. Live it up while you can."

Olson sighed. "I have no time to live it up. And what's so chaotic about you? You're way more organized than I am."

True paused. She squinted at the heart monitor. A few irregular beats, an alarm, then the normal tracing resumed. "I have kids. It's just survival. We can trade for the day and I'll just go chill at your apartment, alone, no offense. You know what it is like when family knows you're a nurse? You'll get this as a doc too. Just wait. This one time about ten years ago I had my mother and her second husband staying with me after she had surgery. Gallbladder. Nothing major. But my house was closer to the hospital and so someone recuperating there for seven days made more sense, right? Jake wasn't born yet and one of the middle boys, Colin, was six. And he was excited that Grandma was visiting.

My mother was just mopping it up. She went from a dilaudid PCA in the hospital that had her looped and calling the physical therapists Laurel and Hardy to taking pills at my house and her sleep cycle was completely off. She was more hyper than the kids."

"That was probably fun for the six year old," said Olson.

"Not even a little bit. You think kids are attention seeking? Grandma wanted all the attention. Mopping up the sympathy. There are women who have grandchildren and dote on them and then there are women who have grandchildren and use every opportunity to undermine their daughters and spaz out the children with candy and then wonder why they won't sit down to dinner.

She was in the living room trying to play chess with Colin. He was always a smart kid and even at six he had the rules pretty well down. She thought she knew the way the pieces moved but she really didn't remember so Colin kept correcting her and he was starting to get annoyed about it. Meanwhile her husband was sleeping on the couch pretending not to be asleep."

"Wouldn't her husband have been your stepdad?" asked Olson.

"Please. They married when I was already thirty. Not a bad guy. But I don't think stepdad was what anyone was looking for at that point. Anyway, he was doing that old guy thing where he's snoring on the couch but will wake up in an instant and insist he wasn't sleeping. Well, we had a terrier mutt at the time. Some hound too, because he could do a really good point. So Grandpa Mike is snoring on the couch and Camel comes in and goes on point, pointing at the snoring guy and holds it for about four minutes. Looks at me, looks at the snoring guy, looks at me, and clearly has no idea what to do next."

"You named your dog Camel?"

"Colin named him Camel because he thought he looked like the Joe the Camel character on my cigarettes."

"You smoke?"

"Used to. Smoke more than I do now. Don't give me that look. Yes, I smoke. Anyways, Camel would have held it for an hour but my mother started shrieking over the chess game that she couldn't breathe and she needed nitro. Colin has seen this act before so he goes to his room to play cars. Mike wakes up and snorts. Camel sits down. Mike rushes to my mother's side and helps her to the door.

She needs air. But not too much air. Because it is raining outside. But she needs nitro. And some water to drink. But he needs to hold her up because she might faint if she doesn't get air. But why is he just standing there? Didn't he hear her say she needed nitro? I swear, the man was a masochist. She had a way of requesting the impossible. Not the impossible like go slay the Jabberwocky, just the really annoying impossible like make the house warmer but not too warm and bring me water that's not too wet.

Meanwhile by now the dog has run outside into the rain. My mother is calling for Colin because of course she needs a bigger audience for the drama, Colin is hiding in his room probably pretending not to hear. I end up bringing her water but I can't find the nitro."

"Was her heart disease that bad?" asked Olson.

"She didn't have any heart disease. She had been worked up the yin-yang for heart disease and it never showed anything but her primary doctor finally prescribed her nitro because it kept her from calling the office every two days with chest pain. The downside is that the rallying cry of 'bring me my nitro' only brought more drama. You could say it in a crowded store and the seas would part, the shopkeeper would bring a footstool for her feet. It worked wonders. It was almost as good as being pregnant."

"She couldn't have been that bad," Olson said.

"If it had happened today I would have just laughed because I would have known what it was. But I still thought there was a kernel of truth to it then. I was a new nurse, I had just enough medical knowledge to worry. There was always that thought of what if I call it crying wolf and she ends up having a big heart attack. After Mike retired, my mother was his project."

"You would be bored without it," said Olson.

"Bored without what?"

"The chaos. Me, my stories are along the lines of, so this one time I was studying and I fell asleep drooling on the book and then here I am."

"That's not so bad," said True. "That's a peaceful existence."

Olson looked down at their patient. "I don't think I'll ever be ready to be responsible for this."

"You'll be fine," said True. "ICU stuff is all protocol based."

"I won't be. I'm terrified of this." Olson sighed. "What's been your hardest case?"

The elevator stopped and the doors opened to another cluster of white coats. They all leaned forward as if to get on and then frowned when they saw the overcrowded car.

"ICU patient," True announced cheerfully.

The doors closed on their frowns.

"This thing is so slow. They must be working on the other one. How about hardest case lately. Did I tell you about the lady with the head laceration?"

Olson shook his head.

True took her eyes off the monitor. "This was the scalp lac to end all lacs. I felt so bad for her. She was eighty-something and very sharp, very with it. Fell. Whacked her head, laid there for who knows how long, long enough to make a mess. This was not just a laceration. This was like some blood spurting alien tomato had attached itself to her head. I mean the doc was up there injecting epinephrine and trying to get some control and it was just swollen and gaped open and spurting. Her shirt was soaked. And the poor thing, she had lain there so long, or passed out from blood loss or something, she'd crapped herself. And she was so embarrassed. She had this Boston accent and she was really hard of hearing so she's shouting about how embarrassed she is that she crapped her drawers. And you know, if you're embarrassed about it maybe shouting is not the best way to talk about it but she couldn't tell.

So finally the doc gets some closure on the head wound and we have her undressed and cleaned up below and there is a trash can full of nasty stuff and she is white as a sheet and needs a blood transfusion. And I just want to go stand under the decon shower and gargle Lysol. And that's when she says 'where's my hearing aid?' and I kind of pretended not to hear her and she said it louder 'where's my hearing aid, it fell out' and I look at the trash full of towels and gauze and I look at the doc and he's just cleaning up the suture tray and about to book out of there. I don't know if he even heard her or not. He asked if I had ever had a shit-storm and a blood bath in the same room before and I told him not. And then he kind of laughs and leaves."

"What did you do?" asked Olson.

True sighed. "Those hearing aids are really expensive. It was probably the most expensive thing she owned. I double-gloved and went through everything. And I found it about two thirds of the way through."

Olson beamed in her presence and stammered as if he didn't know what to say first. "See that's just amazing. You. You are amazing. You're like Mother Theresa on steroids. With tattoos."

"No. I'm not," said True. "Don't say that. I hated it. I hated every minute of it, OK? I wanted to just rifle through it and be done. I wanted to find my nurse intern to do it. It was not amazing. Mother Theresa would have wanted to be there. I wanted to run in the opposite direction."

"But you are amazing. Because you didn't rifle through it. You could have. You could have just said so sad too bad can't find it and nobody would have known."

"I would have known," said True. Then she glared at him. "Don't give me that look. She needed it back. She was a sharp lady. And not having her hearing aid was bugging the crap out of her. No pun intended. But I still hated it. So don't give me that Mother Theresa complex stuff. Some stuff I just do to get through my shift, you know? It puts food on the table at the end of the day but I need to have a relatively clean conscience."

"Relatively?"

"This is not the confessional elevator, Olson. I have my secrets."

Jerry turned to me with a grin. "I told you this was our pair of whistleblowers."

"Why does this clinch it?"

"It's not that I think they have a chance at some romance. Not a chance. But they love to commiserate, buck the system. We can just put the chart right there on this guy," he started to slide it up the rails when the monitor began to alarm.

Olson reached across and turned the screen. He squinted. "Um, True, is that vfib?"

True rolled her eyes. "Yes, you are too young for me. Do you know why? Because you have to ask me if that's vfib. Climb up there."

Olson looked around the elevator compartment, "Climb up where?"

"Climb up next to the patient and start CPR. It's vfib. We're not going to shock him in here. You do CPR and I'll push the bed into the unit where we'll have more help."

"Why don't I push the bed, I bet I'm faster."

"You can't draw up epinephrine or any of the other meds. Besides, do you even know where the unit is from here?"

The door chimed and True wrenched herself behind the bed and pushed it through the slowly opening doors.

"Of course I do, the unit is down the hall past the…umm," stammered Olson.

"Olson, just get up there!" snapped True.

Olson climbed onto the side of the man in the bed and pounded on his sternum.

Jerry grumbled and crossed his arms across his chest.

I watched the CPR with interest this time. The chest wall went down several inches each time and I winced, glad, if I could call it glad, that I had been unconscious for that. The irony. Of course I had been unconscious.

"Jerry, how long did they do that on me?"

"On you? Maybe fifteen minutes or so. And a bunch of shocks."

"That seems like a long time." Then another thought struck me. "Jerry, if they do the garden hose and the ice packs to this guy I think I might pass out."

"You can't pass out if you're dead."

"I don't know. I'm feeling lightheaded just watching this."

"I'm feeling lightheaded watching our opportunity roll away down the hallway."

I sighed. "We may as well follow them," I said.

"This is harder than I thought," said Jerry.

"Come on, I'm not staying in the elevator. What if that guy ends up half-dead too and then we're stuck in the elevator with him?" I said.

"Why, are you afraid of ghosts?"

"I just don't want to meet someone else right now. Anybody. We have enough problems already."

True and Olson were fifty yards down the hall when we left the elevator. The double doors to the intensive care unit were right in front of them. True stood swiping her card over and over and the door would half open and then catch. On the other side there was a group of nurses waving their arms and shouting to push the bed back so the sensor wouldn't over-ride the door. Olson dutifully pounded on the poor guy's chest and tried not to fall off the bed. True finally pulled the bed far enough back that the doors opened.

"Why didn't you call a code overhead?" asked the first nurse.

"We were in the elevator," said True.

"Why did you leave the ER if he was this unstable?" asked the second nurse.

"He wasn't in Vfib when we left the ER."

"Who's that guy," asked the third nurse, pointing at Dr. Olson.

"He's an intern," said True.

The three nurses softened their expressions as if now they understood why True had been unable to accomplish much in the elevator.

Chapter 11

We hurried after them and the doors swung shut. Jerry was nonplussed and glided heedlessly through the door. I could still see him looking at me. He bowed and made a big pantomime of pushing the inside button and the doors finally opened again.

The intensive care unit was laid out in a semicircle with all the patient rooms on the outside and all the work stations in the middle. The noise coming from the other side of the work station made it clear where the new patient was.

"I told you, he was fine when we left the ER. His heart rate was sixty," True told the other nurse.

"That's a little low."

"That's not low. It's normal," said True.

"Normal is sixty to a hundred. He was getting low. You should have picked up on that."

"His heart rate wasn't getting anywhere. It was fine. Then all of a sudden it wasn't," True stammered back.

Intern Olson stepped out of the room. Apparently he had been kicked off CPR duty. "She's right. Sixty is a normal heart rate."

The ICU nurse looked at him. She had those narrow glasses on a beaded chain that magnetically attach at the nose. There was an administrative assistant at Graham and Graham that had a pair like that. She put them together before she said anything in a meeting and then took them apart as soon as she was done. Drove me nuts. "She might be right. But you're not. You should go back in there and do something useful."

Olson slunk back into the patient room and pulled the curtain.

"How did you get stuck with an intern?" asked the ICU nurse.

"That's half of it. I have a nurse intern downstairs too."

The other nurses clucked in sympathy.

"All that and the joint commission is going to be here this week. Have you guys heard when?"

True shook her head. "They usually fly from out of town. Maybe they'll get snowed out of O'Hare if we get a storm tomorrow."

"That would be a relief. I am so sick of having to unlock the drawer to get an IV. Like the intubated ventilator guy in a coma is going to steal IVs and go inject drugs. It is such a pain."

Jerry had caught up with me. I had the sneaking suspicion he had stopped by my room to see how Patient Fries was doing. I had deliberately avoided it.

"Definitely the whistleblowers. He takes himself too seriously and she's just mad at everybody."

"Who, the ICU nurse?"

"Not the ICU nurse. She's just one of those women that wear those glasses. I used to work with a woman like that. What a pain," said Jerry.

I was about to interject about the glasses but he was full steam ahead.

"No, she's not our whistleblower at all. It's True. True's mad at everybody."

"And therefore she'll funnel documents to the board of directors?"

"She's mad because she cares. Remember all the people I told you I didn't like when I was sick. And how she wasn't one of them?"

I smiled at Jerry. The fact that he could be enjoying himself this much was not lost on me. He had said 'when' I was sick as if it was such a long time ago. It reminded me of how my granddaughter Clare referred to things when she was four years old as if it was such a longtime ago. But Jerry's childlike enjoyment did not make me like my situation any better.

"Let's just hand this off and get back to the ER. I've got a bad feeling that guy's ghost is going to walk out from behind the curtain and I just don't want to meet the guy."

"I'm sure he's a nice enough guy," said Jerry. "I wasn't so choosy with you and you're just mildly annoying."

"Thank you, Jerry."

"Why don't you want to meet him?"

I thought for a moment. It wouldn't have made the day any stranger than it already was. "Because it would take up too much time. We have a job to do, remember? If we have to deal with this guy then we'll have to orient him to the hospital. It's like we'd become the welcoming committee. The greeters." What I didn't add was that I didn't want to represent what I was afraid I was a part of. Namely, death.

There were so many doctors and doctors' underlings in the room that Olson was quickly rotated out again. He went and sat next to True in the nursing station.

She was eating more funyuns.

"Where did you get those?"

"In my pocket."

"I thought you were out."

"I was out in the other bag."

They were silent for a moment.

Jerry slid the envelope along the counter and it dropped down to the level where they were sitting.

I held my breath out of habit. I wasn't sure it mattered.

"What is that?" asked the intern.

"I don't know. It says to destroy it."

"Probably patient records. What are you doing?"

Olson reached for it and she turned away from him and kept the envelope just out of reach.

"Opening it. I've been doing this for a while, Olson. I've never seen patients records labeled that way."

"You can't just open it. We should shred it. What if someone sees you?"

"What if someone sees me holding paperwork in my hands in the hospital? I think they won't care. Besides, I'm not going back to the ER right now. Since I stopped smoking I don't get any breaks any more so this is my break. As far as they're concerned I'm still wheeling him to the ICU."

She tore open the envelope and fell silent.

Olson reached for a funyun from the bag and True slapped his hand.

"I told you, I'm on break. Don't interfere with my funyuns break."

"What is it? Is it records from a VIP? I heard the governor was in for a hernia surgery last week."

"Olson, we need to do something about this."

"Something went wrong with the hernia operation? No, don't tell me. He had a sex change operation instead."

"There was no hernia operation. And definitely no sex change operation. We need to do something about this. They're going to close the hospital. They faked the financial reports. Oh my goodness, the CEO has a doctor doing false billing. It's the nursing home doc that always sends his patients in for physical therapy admissions when they're gorked. The director noticed it months ago but I don't think she put two and two together. Olson, this is huge."

The funyuns bag dropped from her other hand.

"This sounds too big for us. We need to turn it in somewhere," he said.

"We can't just turn it in somewhere. Think about this for a minute. Crap."

"Crap what?" asked Olson.

"Crap that I don't want to know about this. I think this is what happened at St. John's. A lot of people lost their jobs too unless you were friends with the right friends."

"Oh come on, True. We're talking about a hospital, not about seventh grade."

"You think people don't lose their jobs for petty reasons? Do you have any idea what's been going on in the ER?"

"Sure. They're renovating it. Starting with the mural."

"They fired most of the doctors and they're replacing them with doctors fresh out of training who'll work without decent malpractice coverage." She held her head in her hands.

"How do you know that?"

True took a deep breath. She looked worried. "Friends. Olson, you need a few life skills or you're going to fall flat on your face when you get your first real job. Were you even around when St. John's closed?"

"Enough about me, what about these papers."

"No really, how old were you when St. John's closed?" She furrowed her brow. "Never mind. Don't tell me, it would just make me depressed."

"I was in school," Olson answered.

"Fine, fine. Don't tell me what grade, ok?" True continued to leaf through the papers. She glanced up to look left and right several times to make sure no one else saw what they were doing. "No. No way I can turn them in," said True.

"Why not?"

"I could lose my job."

Olson had a big grin across his face. "We could be heroes."

True sighed. "We could be heroes on the news for fifteen minutes and then we could be slapped with violation of confidentiality agreements and who knows what else."

"What confidentiality agreements? That's just about patients."

"How many forms did you sign when you started working here? Did you read them all? It's a stacked deck. Believe me. There is some form that you signed in a file somewhere that will screw you over if you tell anyone about this. It's the same way everywhere. You think you own your house until the bank takes it back. You think you have your job until they downsize it and call lay-offs some stupid program that sounds catchy. Except when it happens to a hospital, people can die. People do die. We are so under-staffed already." True was shaking. I watched Olson reach an arm toward her and then stop short as if he thought better of it.

"But you said it yourself. This is big." He took some of the papers and began to flip through them.

"So are my kids. They eat a lot. And I can't afford to lose my job. I already made nice to the new group. Smarmy cheap new boss and all."

"Why cheap?" asked Olson.

"Oh this is a long story. Short version is they invited the nurses out to meet the new group for drinks and appetizers and they switched it to a cash bar at the last minute."

"That is cheap," Olson said.

"You're telling me. It costs twenty bucks to park downtown so a lot of the nurses who brought any cash spent it on that. I went down after a day shift and I was just tired and thought fine, I'll shake hands and have a few beers and pretend it's a night out. Except when I got the bar and ordered they asked for four dollars. Not only did they make it a cash bar, someone from the management called and made it a cash bar like two hours before the meet and greet was supposed to start."

"Wow," Olson said. "You know, even in college if I had friends over I'd usually spring for the beer. What would it have cost them for a few pitchers per table? A hundred bucks?"

"Well, probably a lot more than that. We're ER nurses, Olson. We drink. But the principle is the same. Anyways, no point getting into all that. The point is the cheap boss is my new boss and I don't want to make waves."

"It wouldn't make waves with the new boss, he doesn't have anything to do with this," Olson said.

"Yes it would. Waves are waves. But what I don't understand is why the envelope was just sitting here."

"That is a little weird," said Olson.

"And they're in the envelope all organized. Olson, somebody left it here to be found."

"So somebody else is the whistleblower but they're too scared to do it," said Olson. "I'm telling you, this is our big moment."

"That's enough of the 'our' stuff. My big moment is when my paycheck shows up twice a week. I pay the bills and put gas in the car and in the summer the kids go to boy scout camp at a discount because I'm the camp nurse. That's all the excitement I need."

"But if this is true and they close St. Augustine's, you'll still be out of a job. What if we save it? We'll save all the jobs not to mention keeping this place running in the middle of the city."

True shook her head. "That's the problem though. Look at the notes here. If this is true and the CEO was double-counting, if the numbers get corrected, this hospital will be almost sixty million dollars in the red. I think its closing is a matter of time."

"But we can't let her get away with this," said Olson. "If this goes down the way it looks, she'll close the hospital and still walk away with a big payday."

"Yes, we can. I can. I do not need to be labeled as a whistle-blower. It makes it just as hard to land the next job after that because people think you're trouble."

"Then I'll do it. I'll take it to the media. I'll copy it and mail it anonymously"

"You can't do it anonymously. They'll need more evidence than they have here."

"I'll wear somebody else's coat while I do it. The long coats all have the names embroidered on them. I could borrow one from Dr. Leak. You know that guy? He's kind of an ass. Then he could take the heat if there is some confidentiality thing."

"That wouldn't work. You couldn't keep it up. Besides, what if you ended up on TV? Someone would recognize you."

"Who should I give this to?" he asked.

True drummed her fingers nervously on the counter. Jerry and I leaned in toward them, waiting. "You really want to do this?"

"Absolutely," said Olson.

"I think the best people to see it would be the board of directors. They hired the CEO. They answer to the Sisters of Charity nuns. They're ultimately the ones who get embarrassed if the story hits the news. But maybe the news needs to see it at the same time. Then they have to really investigate the story. Investigate beyond what's here," said True.

Jerry nodded vigorously and grinned.

"Beyond what's here? There's a lot here," said Olson.

"There is but what if the CEO claims they aren't her emails? Somebody printed up things that have her email signature but it's all on paper. She could deny it. For eleven million dollars and more at stake she probably will. See, this is why whistleblowers usually bite the dust. Forget it. Olson, this is crazy. We need to leave this envelope here and just walk away."

I was biting my lip. True was a good person. I could see her point. I certainly didn't want her to get into trouble. It was easy enough for Jerry and me to push this. We were safely out of reach. Well, he was. I hoped to be back to normal soon. I glanced around the ICU to where Patient Fries was in his room. I didn't see anyone familiar outside the glass door. This is what happens, I thought. The good people like True are trapped by the system. The merely average people like myself don't realize what they need to do until it's too late.

It was maddening. To have such a cliché thrust in my face and to be able to do nothing about it. Maybe the best I could do was start writing essays and hope someone would find them. They would be short and repetitive. Seize the day. You might drop dead in someone's living room. You never know when. And then that's it. Simple. No trumpet fanfare. No angels at the gate. You'll meet an old guy in rumpled corduroy and wait for the bureaucracy to sort itself out. And then it will really be over. A sputter out. And if you have regrets all you can do is kick yourself with your ghostly foot and you won't feel the impact no matter how hard you kick.

I was so wrapped up in moping that I almost missed Jerry turning to follow Olson and True, who were walking toward the exit door.

"True, where are you taking the envelope?" Olson asked.

"To the board of directors."

"What? I thought you said to forget about it?"

True shook her head. "Olson, don't you get anything? Of course we have to turn this in. It's just another example of my crappy luck to have it land in my lap."

"You're going to turn it in?"

"No. We are going to turn it in but I need your help in figuring out how to do it."

"What's with the we stuff?"

"Don't get any ideas. Come on. Let's go save the day."

True still sounded pretty sarcastic to me, but she was carrying the envelope. Jerry looked back at me and waved me to follow.

They had nearly reached the elevator when Olson stopped walking suddenly. "Shoot," he said. "I have a conference with my advisor. I can't miss it. It might take an hour. Dr. Chawala. It might take more."

"Never heard of him," True replied.

"He hardly ever sees patients, that's why. He just runs the residency program, talks about his glory days in the Indian army, and drives the residents nuts. You know how to use the paging system, right?"

"Of course," True said.

Olson scribbled a number on a piece of paper. "This is my pager number. Can you page me in about twenty minutes?"

"Are you trying to get my number again?" True asked.

"No. Just page me in twenty minutes, OK?"

"Why?"

"Because Chawala will be twenty minutes into his story on this one case of tuberculosis he had twenty years ago and I will be about to lose my mind."

"Then you have to hang on to the paperwork. If I bring it with me, I'll lose it in the ER or somebody will see it."

"Deal," said Olson, taking the envelope.

I looked toward Jerry and he nodded. We followed the intern down the hall and True headed into the elevator.

Olson went into an office marked "Educational Administration" and we followed. There were five students around the table or perhaps they were interns. I couldn't tell. Everyone wore short coats and had folders bulging with paperwork with them. Olson joined them at the table. He took the wasabi peas out of his coat pocket, opened them and left them in the middle of the table. One of the students on the other side made a face. "Is that your contribution to the session?"

Olson smiled. "They aren't for you."

"Don't worry. I don't want any. They look stale anyways."

The room was lined by shelving on two sides that was covered with trophies. Most were ornate, several tiers high, some topped by the figure of a gilded man, a few topped by an eagle, each with a plaque along a common theme, "Best Residency Director, Dr. Chawala." I think they must have come from a bowling league store. I was curious to see this guy.

Jerry was over by the far wall, reading the trophies and chuckling to himself.

"Students, I am sorry to be running late. I had a very important meeting just before this and then I stopped to get some x-rays to show you. I have some very unique, very historical and significant examples of tuberculosis seen on chest x-ray. Dr. Olson will be beginning this session with a case report. Dr. Olson, are you ready with your presentation?" Dr. Chawala settled into the arm chair in front of the wasabi peas. He was about seventy years old, portly, neatly dressed in a charcoal suit and a light blue striped tie.

Olson fished through his stack of papers, dropped the envelope on the floor, quickly grabbed it back, and found the report he was looking for. He cleared his throat and began. "This patient was admitted through the emergency department three days ago. She is a thirty-five year old female who presented with right lower quadrant pain, nausea, and low grade fevers for about twelve hours."

"Stop right there," Dr. Chawala blurted. "You must define your terms. Where is the right lower quadrant? What does nausea mean? It means different things to different people. What was her actual temperature? One cannot be so cavalier."

"I was about to get into that," Olson interjected.

"You know, young man, when I was an officer in the Indian Army, things were different. One had to define their terms absolutely. There was no room for generalities. I am sure you are going to go over a case of appendicitis, or perhaps some pathology of the ovary and then discuss the work up of right lower quadrant pain in the female. An excellent topic for this type of session. Very bread and butter medicine, as they say. But what I am looking for in the residents is an exploration of the art, a probing of the craft. Only when I am sure that you know what nausea means can you simply say that someone had nausea for twelve hours. You have not defined a single thing yet in this case report!" Dr. Chawala drummed his fingers on the table and they brushed the bag of wasabi peas.

"Sir, if I may continue…" Olson said.

"Nausea emanates from many sources. It might be dizziness for someone. It might be from pathology in the brain stem. We must not be too hasty in marching down a mental rut that leads us to appendicitis. I was on an exercise once that led us high into the mountains. Many more meters in elevation than any of us had ever climbed," he reached down and sampled some of the wasabi peas. "The younger men in the company had not prepared for the altitude to change the weather but of course it was very cold at such elevation," he continued, eating a few more of the wasabi peas.

Jerry returned to my side, having made the rounds of the various trophies. "Listening to this guy talk, I think these trophies are a joke. Can't blame the students really. His ego's big enough to believe it and they need to have a little fun. What's he eating?"

"Wasabi peas. Olson put them on the table."

"What the heck is that?"

"They're spicy," I said. "It's the bag our genius picked up downstairs the first time we tried to give him the envelope."

"He went for stale snack food. At least he wasn't taking it for himself," Jerry said, shaking his head.

"What do you mean," I asked.

"Watch."

Dr. Chawala took another handful as he regaled the stone-faced students about his exploits at high altitude. Olson had already folded up his presentation and put it back in his pocket, apparently aware that he was not going to get another word in edgewise. His pager beeped and he quickly got up from the table and left the room. While he was gone two other interns' pager went off and they passed Olson in the doorway as he returned. "The page out, nice going," said one in passing. "Who did you get to start it?"

"One of the nurses in the ER," Olson answered.

"I owe you."

"You'll owe me more if he finishes that bag."

"How old are those anyway?"

"At least four years old."

"That's amazing. Where did you get them?"

"I cannot reveal my sources," Olson replied.

Dr. Chawala called to his receptionist. There was no answer. "She must have stepped out. Excuse me, I must get some water. They keep doing work on the plumbing, you know, turning it on and off. I would recommend you all avoid the drinking fountains for the next few days. I must go to the break room refrigerator. Look over your notes, Dr. Olson, and we will continue your case when I return." He passed the two interns coming back into the office just as the beepers on another two went off.

One of the young men across the table looked at Olson in amazement. "I never realized you could do that."

Olson smiled. "The page out? It's as old as pagers. And much easier than getting someone to page you overhead. Be careful when you use it though. Save it for desperate times only."

"How did you know he would eat the wasabi peas?"

"Just wishful thinking. But after the last grand rounds when he took the last chocolate chip cookie and the jalapeno chips before the students even went through the buffet line, I thought either the man has no shame or he would eat anything."

"You are giving me hope to survive my internship next year, bro."

Jerry was beaming, at least I think he was beaming. It was hard to tell through his thick eyebrows. But he was smiling at Olson.

"Do you think their professor really deserved that?" I asked.

"Probably," Jerry said.

"Probably? I'm surprised at you," I said.

"Really? You never had a blow hard like that in your line of work? Let me tell you about this one tax season back in 1982. Bad example maybe, but I'm trying to think of something interesting in the accounting field. We spent ten minutes in here and he's already telling war stories. I've been stuck with you for how many hours and I've told you what, maybe one war story? Maybe two? And those were for your education, not just to hear myself talk. It's no wonder they give this guy bowling trophies."

"You think they're bowling trophies too? I wondered that but I never have really seen a bowling trophy," I said.

Jerry went on as if he hadn't heard me. "I hope I wasn't one of those old guys that was always talking about how great it was back in the day. It wasn't. We had the draft, the highway system was lousy, the motels were worse, McCarthyism reared its head and by the time I was old enough to really have a say it was the sixties. Of course of lot of things are worse today. Resilience is down. Men can make a cappuccino but they can't fix a lawn mower engine.

Nobody wants to hear war stories unless they were in the war with you. Memories are for the people you made them with."

Jerry was looking out the window toward the south side of the city and he looked miles away.

"You've probably never been to the Avalon. Neighborhood might have been too rough for you to come to the south side from way out in the burbs. Not guns like it is now. But a guy could get knifed in a stick-up every once in a while. But it's an example. I wouldn't tell anyone about the Avalon except the people that used to go there. To them, to me, it was a great theatre. Classy. Made to look like a Mediterranean city with little terraces painted on the walls. I went there a couple times as a kid, before the war. First place I ever went to see a picture. I used to look up at those terraces, look at the columns, and think rich people must have had apartments up there and they got to watch the movies from their balconies. It was all just paint and plaster but they dimmed the lights and it was part of the magic.

We went there after the war too and then you could drink and they expanded to a bar and restaurant before you went to see the picture. I was there with Spike and this girl came up and she got nervous and asked him 'do you frequent here often' and something about it was funnier than it really was, you know? We laughed about it for a month. He'd tell me to meet him somewhere and I'd ask if it was that place he frequented often and it would start again.

So anyways, it closed a couple of years ago. Neighborhood went from rough to really rough. Open almost a hundred years, not quite. But that's how it goes. Am I supposed to carry a sign and join the historical society and march? It meant a lot to me and Spike and I took Millie there a couple times. But to anyone else? We're all ghosts now. We may as well have been ghosts when it closed. There's a lot of places like that. You can't go back. I don't think the professor gets that or he wouldn't still be bragging about how many times he climbed mount whatsit."

"Who's Spike?" I asked.

"My brother," Jerry said. "Nickname."

"Is he, is he still," I stammered.

"He died in Korea."

"I'm sorry" I said.

"Long time ago," Jerry said. "Different place almost. You can't tell a kid anything. Couldn't tell Spike anything. He was a hell-raiser. My younger brother. Good looking kid. The girls loved him. I always had to get him out of trouble. There was still a draft for that one but they weren't taking everybody. I tried to get him to go to college and see if it could be deferred but he wouldn't listen to me. Wanted to do his time in the service like his big brother. It seemed like it wasn't long after that my son got drafted." Jerry fell silent and looked out the office window as if he was miles away. Then he crossed the room and looked into the reception area. "No sign of Professor Koala. Let's see if these guys do anything useful," he gestured at Olson and the rest of the crew. Two of the interns were dozing off in their chairs.

Olson seemed to have the same idea. He stood next to Jerry at the door. "Listen guys, can you cover me if he comes back? If he's not back in ten minutes I think we're all clear, but if he does, can you say I got paged back to the ER?"

The other interns, those who were awake at least, nodded agreement. Olson left with his bundle of cases and the envelope.

Chapter 12

Olson made his way back to the ER without running into Dr. Chawala. He caught sight of True and Dr. Maglio and pulled up a chair by the radiology computers. Jerry and I followed.

"Are you going to give her haldol or anything?" True asked Maglio.

"The one in sixteen? I probably should. I was kind of enjoying her stream of consciousness though."

"Let me rephrase that. I have to go in and draw blood for an alcohol level and whatever else you need to clear her for a mental health bed and I don't need her to be singing and crying at the same time while I'm trying to get an IV. So can you order up some haldol, please, doc?" asked True.

There was a torrent of words from behind the curtain of room sixteen. "I am never going back to being fat. Never. Never. The kids don't appreciate me. I'm going to sing. I'm going to make it big. I can laugh all the way to the bank. I lost a hundred pounds and did they put me on TV? No. Did they give me a singing job? No. But I'm not a slob. Slob. Never. I am never going back."

Olson raised an eyebrow at True. "What's her deal?"

"We usually see her in the summer. She had weight loss surgery and lost a bunch of weight but now she has some loose skin, you know, because of the rapid weight loss. Definitely has some body issues. She's a teacher and she tends to get loaded in the summer. We usually see her a bunch then. This time it must be the winter holidays. I think she's supposed to be on lithium or something. She gets delusional and drunk and we never know which came first."

There was loud singing and occasional bursts of tears from behind the curtain.

"You are all so beautiful. You understand. The kids at school, they saw my arms and asked what 'that' was and they were pointing at my skin."

Maglio shook his head. "Someone who still has issues with what the kids at school think probably shouldn't be a teacher. Give her five of haldol."

"We don't have an IV yet, can I give a shot?"

"Whatever works," muttered Maglio.

"She's really a teacher?" Olson was incredulous.

"Oh we get a lot of drunk teachers in the summer. Usually not this loony. Wouldn't you need to tie one on if you had their job?" Maglio said.

Paula the secretary had stood up and left her post. She was holding her own middle with two hands showing off her rather developed belly roll.

"She needs to be quiet in there or I'm going to march in there and show her some of this," she said, jiggling her roll for emphasis. "I like to eat and there's nothing wrong with a little of this. And if I go show her this it just might kill her for real. So Maglio, will you please give her something to make her be quiet?"

Maglio's expression was pained. "Keep it covered, got it, she'll get some haldol."

I followed Olson's gaze. There was a team wheeling someone on a ventilator to the scanner. Behind them were two cops taking turns talking with a half naked guy in handcuffs wearing a shredded purple sequined dress and a cowboy hat. I looked closer. Same guy from earlier but different cops, I was pretty sure. Overhead the paging system barked out a code blue on one of the telemetry floors and the row of monitors beeped incessantly to Maglio's right.

"Her job can't be that bad," stammered Olson.

"Speaking of bad jobs, here, take this," Maglio slid a Med Prompt receiver across the counter toward the intern. "I want you to answer my calls for a while."

"I get to use your Med Prompt?" asked Olson.

"With great power comes great responsibility," said Maglio. "Just push the big button to log in." He checked his watch and left his chair.

"Med prompt. Please say or spell your name," said the receiver.

Olson put his lips right next to the speaker. "Dr. Olson."

"OK," said the receiver cheerfully, "I'm logging you in as Ken Haversham."

"That's not right," said Olson.

"Med Prompt. Let's try again. Please say or spell your name."

This time he over-enunciated. "Doctor Olson."

"I didn't understand. Med Prompt. I am recalculating. Med Prompt. Please say or spell your name."

Maglio returned from the staff lounge a few moments later carrying the bagel bag.

"Dr. Maglio, wait. This thing won't let me log in," said Olson.

"Sure it will. It's easy to use. We all use them."

Olson turned red and sheepishly walked almost out of earshot. "Dr. Olson," he said again.

"Med Prompt," came the reply, "I am calling pharmacy for a dose of IV zosyn, please say or spell the dose."

"Incorrect," pleaded Olson.

"I heard you say direct," said the receiver. "Med Prompt. That is not a valid order. Please log in to place pharmacy order. Please say or spell your name."

True left Olson to argue with the med prompt for a while and zeroed in on the bagel bag in Maglio's hand. She was about to say something when the doors swung open and a young man briskly walked through, red faced and carrying a paper bag. Alvarez was right behind him. "Sir. I'll get her but you need to calm down and tell me what this is about."

"I just need to talk to Angie."

"I need to know what's in the bag," Alvarez continued.

"I need to see my wife," the other man shouted.

Maglio headed in the same direction. "True, I'll be back in ten minutes. Olson's taking my calls. The urology clinic is just down the outpatient hall."

The nurse intern peeked her head out from the curtain in room four. "Honey, what are you doing here?" she asked the man holding the bag.

"Was this some kind of joke?" he asked her, shaking the Genius Bagel bag in front of him.

True was between them before either could say another word.

"I just love bagels!" she said loudly, twisting the bag out of his hands. "Dr. Maglio, you must have gotten lunch at the same place," she added, stepping on front of him as he tried to walk past.

The nurse intern's husband stammered. "Angie, you need to explain something."

"Yes indeed, Dr. Maglio, looks like you have the same bag. What a coincidence," True hissed.

"Why did you bring Zoey's milk back?" the nurse intern asked her husband.

"True, I told you where I'm going. This isn't lunch," Maglio growled.

"But it might be someone's lunch. You never know," True pointed her chin toward the other man.

"True, what in the world are you doing?" Maglio tried to step past her.

"Maglio, give me the bag," True said.

"Can't a man deliver a sperm sample in peace around here?" Maglio asked.

He moved left and True countered, still holding the other bag out of reach of the nurse intern's husband. "Is this yours?" the husband asked.

Maglio was still puzzled. "That's not my bag. This is my bag," he jerked it over True's head who nearly grabbed it.

"You might want to check," the husband said.

Now True was pushing both men toward the door. "Just trade. Just trade and go about your business."

Maglio started to laugh. He opened the bag in his hand and laughed louder. "Sorry, man. Here you go." He turned to the nurse intern. "Becky, I didn't mean to embarrass you."

"What are you even talking about? Embarrass me about what? My name is Angie, anyways."

True had her arm around the husband's shoulder as he turned lobster red. She shoved the other bagel bag at Maglio. "We're sort of one big happy family here. Things get mixed up in the fridge sometimes. You know how that goes with a work fridge. Somebody takes your sandwich, somebody leaves something in there for three weeks, nobody likes to clean it, breast milk gets confused with a sperm sample, just your typical work fridge. So nice of you to come see Angie. She is doing such a nice job on her internship."

"So if you work here you have to pump in the same room somebody whacks off in? What kind of working conditions are these? I think my wife should file a complaint," the husband said.

"For the record, I whacked off at home and just needed the fridge to store the sample," said Maglio.

"That's disgusting," said the husband. "This is a hostile work environment."

"Tell me about it," chimed Alvarez.

"Angie and I are trying to keep Zoey healthy. We believe in breastfeeding for as long as possible. I'm working part-time so Angie can finish this internship and she has to come to work and deal with this? Do you think this is some kind of joke? This is bordering on harassment."

Maglio cleared his throat. He looked at the other man square in the eye. "I don't know you sir, and I am a rather private person. But I feel I must share the fact that the reason why you carried home my sperm sample by mistake is that my wife and I are trying to have a child. I need to get this over to the clinic immediately and I hope, I just hope, that the fertility pills I've been taking will have finally done their magic and I can go home tonight and tell my wife that I'm no longer," Maglio coughed for effect, "that I'm no longer shooting blanks. If you'll excuse me, I always get choked up when I talk about this. I need to go."

He strode away and the doors closed behind him with a quiet hydraulic hiss. Angie stepped closer to her husband. "It's not a bad place to intern, honey. They don't really whack off in the lounge. But the fridge is pretty gross."

"I'm sorry," her husband said. "Tell that guy I'm sorry I overreacted. I kind of left this bag on the dash while I drove here too. Do you think the heater might have killed some? I don't want him to get a false reading just because of me."

"I'm sure he has plenty of sperm," said True.

"Fertility pills and everything, man, that's hard. I hope they make it," said Angie's husband.

Angie turned toward True. "I never knew they made fertility pills for men."

True was staring at the closed exit doors and shaking her head. "It's a new thing. I think it's experimental. Dr. Maglio was always one to volunteer for a cause."

Alvarez stared at the exit doors. "Man, for all we knew, he could have had a gun in that bag. We can't just buzz anyone back who says so and so works here."

"If it had been a gun, it would have been loaded with blanks," True replied.

"OK, no more discussion of Maglio's wang. The man talks about it enough while he's here," said Alvarez. "I'm serious about this. This ER needs better security."

"Careful who you say that in front of; you might talk yourself out of a job," said True.

The director looked up from her computer. "Don't worry. Your job is secure for the next fifteen days before the contract officially expires."

"Thanks, doc."

"Don't mention it. You know what the last patient I saw said? I asked her how she was doing and she said, I don't know, you tell me. And that was all she said. She forgot why she called 911. You could try that in interviews. Why do I want to work here? I don't know, you tell me. It's a great answer to a lot of questions if you think about it. I just want the holidays to be over."

"But there are, what is today, January fifteenth?"

"That still counts as the holidays. Holiday hang over, dealing with relatives, it all spills over into the ER and people call 911 just to get out of the house."

"They don't really do that, do they?" asked Olson.

"They call to get out of jail, to avoid going to jail, why not to avoid dealing with houseguests that won't leave? I've been tempted. You heard about the guy who was faking heart attacks to avoid paying his restaurant bill, right? We busted him right here. He had made five ambulances trips this year with the same scam and he finally broke down and bragged about it to one of our docs. Called police and the guy left in cuffs from the ER. But my point is, the drama from the holidays doesn't go away until February. Look at the tracking board. Look at all the chief complaints."

Olson read through them. "Short of breath, chest pain, diarrhea, constipation, tingling and numbness, diarrhea, dizzy, chest pain again, what does this have to do with holiday fallout?"

"If you go talk to them, everyone is here due to anxiety," the director said.

"Even the guy with constipation?" Olson asked.

"Especially that guy. Should go meet him. He's probably great at parties. I rarely use the phrase anal-retentive to describe a personality but he fits it. And his wife, or girlfriend, or whoever is in there with him, is actually wearing a shirt that says 'control freak' on it. Yes, truth is stranger than fiction. Are you having a good rotation here, by the way?"

"Sure, it's a good rotation. Thanks."

"By the way, there are some real patients here. They're the ones with diarrhea. There's a nasty stomach bug going around. Make sure to wash your hands," she said.

"OK."

"You know the joint commission is going to be here sometime this week, right?"

"I've heard that."

"Do you mind if I send you to the committee and have you answer all their questions?"

"Me?" asked Olson incredulously.

"She's messing with you," said True.

Olson looked disappointed. "I could listen in. I have an interest in administration."

"You'll lose that interest if you go to a joint commission evaluation. They'll ask to review a case and you'll bust out the best trauma save of the week, the multiple gun shots that got a thoracotomy and bedside splenectomy and got wheeled upstairs to recovery already doing the crossword puzzle and the reviewers will close the case and ask you how many fire extinguishers are between here and the room the patient went to. And then you'll consider setting fire to the file. Then your attention will drift and you'll wonder how your retirement investments are doing and if you retired to the third world right now would you have enough to live on. And then you'll remember that you don't give a flying freak because the contract is ending. Don't mind me, Olson. Just enjoy the month."

"OK," said Olson. "Thanks."

"And if you do set anything on fire, do it in room sixteen. That seems to be where that always happens."

Maglio came back from his errand minus the bagel bag. He sat down by the radiology computers which were back in service despite Jerry's best efforts at cross-wiring all the plugs. He wasn't mumbling about Wangs anymore.

"How are the swimmers?" asked the director.

"Geez, you're as bad as my wife. I'm surprised she hasn't called again. I'll find out in a day or two."

"What's with the pizza?" asked the director.

Maglio had an oversized slice poised over the keyboard, dripping.

"It's dinner," he said simply.

"With the joint commission coming through?"

"Do you want me to get enough for the whole department?" he asked.

The director grinned. "I'll think about that."

"I don't think they're coming through today anyways. I just saw the CEO in the hall. She's leading a suits parade but I think it's the board, not the commission."

Jerry was beside himself.

"This might be it. This might be our chance. Let's hope they don't blow it. Come on over here," he motioned to me.

True and Intern Olson were huddled by the chart rack.

"Where's the file?" True asked him.

"Why?"

"Didn't you just hear the director? The CEO is headed to the ER on a suits tour with the board of directors. We can give it to them."

"I'm not handing it over in front of all of them!"

"You have to!"

"No way. Too many people. They'll crucify us. Whistleblowers don't fare well, remember? You told me that how many times? We need a sympathetic ear."

"What happened to ethics and saving the hospital?" True asked.

"I just don't want to hand it over to all of them at once."

"Well, if you won't do it, I will. Give me the file."

"I could create a diversion while you do. Then they won't know where it came from. Do you want me to fake a seizure?" Olson asked.

True wasn't buying it. "Where is the file?"

The intern reached into his coat pocket and frowned. He turned his chair around and looked on the counter. "I must have put it in a chart."

"Oh for God's sake, find the file."

I didn't know who to kick first, the intern or myself for choosing this guy to get the information. Olson started on the left side of the rack and began pulling out the plastic binders. He rifled through each one while True glared at him. But before I could join the search for the chart, an eruption of noise came from room four.

"You can't take that stuff."

"Don't you know its cold out there?"

Alvarez the security guard flung the curtain back and poked his head out. "A little help in here."

Raymond was awake. He had sobered up enough to get out of bed and get his coat on and he was stuffing his coat, half-zipped, with a hospital blanket, handfuls of washcloths, and the envelopes upon envelopes of paper from his chart.

"You can leave but you can't take that stuff."

"Do you want me to die? Do you want me to freeze? You are heartless, man."

"Raymond, calm down. We'll send you to the mission."

"No. No mission. They telling me about God don't want me to drink. They worried about my soul. Bull. They worried about my soul they can give me something to drink. If those holy rollers cared about anything other than themselves they would give a thirsty man a drink. God made the grape. God made the grape and turned water to wine."

"You can drink all you want, man, you just can't stay here," said Alvarez.

"Don't you touch me you heathen rent a cop," Raymond yelled.

Alvarez rolled his eyes. "They don't pay me enough."

The double doors swung open and the procession of suits came down the hall. Belle Evans was flanked by the board and she paused by the mural. "We're just beginning the process but this is one example of the beautification of St. Augustine's. Of course when we break ground for a larger emergency department we'll be able to expand our services to the community even more."

"You know me. I'm Raymond Ray all day long. I don't need none of this."

Raymond had made it past the room four doors and Alvarez was following at a safe distance, still calling for help. "I need back up security in the ER. Back up security code green."

The director and Maglio watched the whole procession. "They have a term for this, you know," she said.

"A term for what?" asked Maglio.

"A term for the fact that our one security guard has to call for back up and the backup isn't going to come. They are calling it pathways to excellence. It's what they named the staffing cuts."

"Let me guess, the med exec meeting was scintillating today?"

"Actually it wasn't as bad as usual. I dropped the bomb that only one of our docs signed with the new group and that the new grads are on their way. And I think I mentioned the lack of malpractice insurance as being a factor."

"You might have just let that slip into the conversation?"

"I think I just might have."

"How did that go over?" Maglio asked.

"It took on a life of its own."

One of the maintenance men came through the doors and eased past the congregation by the mural. He walked directly to the secretary's desk. I couldn't quite make out what he said over Raymond's protests.

The parade remained at a standstill at the mural. The CEO seemed hesitant to continue into the ER. "Of course we serve a challenging patient population," the CEO said, backing into the phalanx of board members.

"Come on Raymond, just give back the blankets," Alvarez coaxed.

"Come and get them, rent-a-cop. Heathen. Heartless heathen. Want me to freeze."

Alvarez glanced at the CEO. "We don't let you take hospital property, sir. You need to give back the blankets. Just give them back and we'll help get you a warm bed for the night."

"Don't sir me, cop! I told you I'm not going to the mission."

"I just remembered where I put the files," the intern blurted. I turned back toward him. "True, they're in Raymond's chart."

True growled something in reply and pointed to the empty room four slot in the chart rack. "Did you leave the chart in the room?"

"Crap," he headed into room four.

The CEO was trying to regain her composure for the tour and smiled her veneers as the intern dashed by. "One of our great strengths is our role as a teaching hospital. We know our patients get excellent care from the residents and students in training. They are a vital and integrated part of the team throughout St. Augustine's. The emergency department staff have also all undergone de-escalation training. This allows them to calm down potentially violent patients without the use of restraints and we were able to cut our security staffing hours by just over thirty percent for a significant cost savings. Not to mention it is much more humane for the patients who have these unfortunate mental or substance abuse ailments. And of course we want to create a pleasant atmosphere for all our patients in the hospital."

"You touch me and I'll kill you," shouted Raymond.

Alvarez keyed his radio and message boomed overhead through the PA system. "Any available security officer, any available security officer, please report to the ER immediately. Repeat. Please report to the ER immediately."

"True, it's not here," Olson shouted.

"What's not there?" she shouted back. "Your stethoscope?" she shouted again. "Keep it down," she hissed back.

He came out of the room. "I think it's in his coat."

Alvarez shouted toward the intern. "What's in his coat?"

"His chart," said Olson.

"Olson's stethoscope," said True, glaring at the intern. They both stepped closer to Raymond.

"Why would he take his chart and your stethoscope? Raymond. You can't take your chart home. And you need to give the doctor back his stethoscope."

Raymond clutched his coat tighter. "Not my chart. No, this is confidential. Shit. I'm not that drunk. This is classified. I'm going to call the president and then the FBI and then the Marines. Then maybe I can get fifty-seven million dollars too. Confidential. I read it. Fifty-seven million. Medicalidocious. I got to go. You get it, you might destroy it, just like it says. You a sheep in that white coat."

One board member in the back furrowed his brows at the specific number.

"Come on Raymond, just give it back."

"Sheeple, sheeple, sheeple," he shouted.

"Raymond, don't do that," True raised the alarm but it was too late. He was urinating on the wall.

The director frowned at Dr. Maglio. "You know he always pees on something if we don't kick him out in time. Normally I'd ask you why you didn't discharge him sooner but I'm kind of glad today that you didn't."

"Well if he didn't christen the mural I was going to have to do it myself," said Maglio.

The CEO turned red and turned to Alvarez. "Officer, aren't you going to do something?"

Alvarez did his best impression of standing at attention. "It's best to wait until he's done and puts it away ma'am. Less of a mess."

"Wait until he's done? Puts it away? Are you crazy?" she blustered.

Just then a young woman came out of the restroom in the same hallway. She was leading her daughter by the hand. She raised her other hand to get Alvarez' attention. "I'm sorry sir. I can see you're busy. Just wanted to let you know the toilet won't flush in here. She's here with the stomach flu and well, I'm sorry about the mess. The sink doesn't work either…" her voice trailed off as she took in the vision that was Raymond.

Raymond zipped up and started for the door. Alvarez and the intern ran after him. Olson grabbed Raymond's left arm and Raymond promptly punched him in the jaw with his free right hand. Olson fell, grabbing his own jaw in pain as Alvarez caught up, tripping over the intern's flailing legs. But Alvarez grabbed the front of Raymond's jacket to break his fall and the ancient zipper readily gave way. Raymond was down, half on top of the Olson, and an explosion of papers erupted out of the coat. They fell like leaves over the board of directors.

I watched Jerry move into the melee, kicking at some of the errant papers, gathering a few others in his hands and tossing them again in the direction of the board members. I tried to picture what it must have looked like to those who couldn't see him, just a whirling dervish of paper. The same man in the grey flannel suit who had noticed some of the particulars of Raymond's rant collected some of the sheets and motioned to his colleagues to do the same…

Chapter 12

The feeling of an endotracheal tube coming out of one's own throat is probably one of the worst things to experience in medicine. Actually one of the worst things to experience in the world. On par with the garden hose. Although thinking about it I realized I still had that in place and chances are I would be awake when they pulled it out. At least I was unconscious when they put the damn thing down. Not unconscious exactly. More like dead. But even though I wasn't awake completely, I did feel that reverse gag as the plastic tube slid out. I coughed, it felt like about a hundred times, to the tune of distant voices saying "Take some deep breaths. Deep breaths. Good job, Mr. Fries, you're doing great."

"It doesn't rhyme with French-fries. It rhymes with cheese. Just call me cheese. Everyone else does," I said hoarsely.

I still couldn't see anything clearly although there was some light and movement in front of my eyes. More voices, more urgent. "He's talking!"

"Did you hear that? He made a joke."

"That's not a joke. That's a sensitive issue. He never likes to be called Cheese, has he lost his mind?"

"Don't worry, it's normal for there to be some confusion when someone comes out of a coma."

Now I could make out a face clearly and I finally heard a familiar voice.

"We got em. Wait until you see the news this morning."

"Jerry?"

"Can you see me?"

"I can see you. What happened?"

"You vanished right out of the ER. Raymond had the envelope in his coat. He clobbered the intern and the security guard. The papers went sailing, right on top of the board of directors and poof, you disappeared. I figured you were either really dead or on your way back."

"Where am I?"

"Back in your old bod and waking up in the ICU."

"But I can still see you. I must be dead."

Jerry laughed.

"Oh my god, he's hallucinating."

"Don't worry. This is normal. He's coming around. Keep taking deep breaths Mr. Fries."

"He's having visions. He thinks he's dead. He must see the face of God."

"It's far from normal. It's a miracle."

"Honey, do you see a light? Don't go toward the light. Stay with us."

Jerry laughed louder and other voices faded.

"You're not dead. How do you feel?"

I coughed again. "Like crap."

"There you go. Proof that you're alive. Anyway, you'll see it this morning. We got em. The board must have read the file cover to cover. One guy, he started looking at it right in the ER. That CEO is toast."

"How long have I been here?"

"About three days."

"Three days! What have you been doing?"

"What have I been doing? Do you think I don't know how to have fun in this place without you around to grandstand and complain? I've been doing what I set out to do before you got me involved in this caper. Haunting the nurses' locker room."

"I wouldn't even try to teach you new tricks."

"They have a big TV in there too so I kept up with the news."

"The news?" I asked, coughing again.

"Yes, the news. It's all over the news. Geez Alan, this coma made you dense. You need to snap out of it."

"I'm not feeling that snappy. Crappy is more like it, I told you that right?" I tried to smile and my face hurt. My throat was so dry it felt like my tonsils were wearing mittens. "How was the locker room anyways?"

"Gets old. Not that many cute nurses after all. The scrubs hide a lot. I miss Millie. Leak and Maglio got into it over not just what the definition of death is but what the definition of 'is' is so now the director requested a copy of my chart from medical records and it's just a matter of time before it's signed."

"Jerry, you can't go."

Jerry laughed. "Alan, need I remind you, I died the same day you did. Remember? Now, if you'll excuse me, I need to pay a visit to True downstairs." He patted his jacket where another envelope peaked out. "A little something for her sons."

"What is that?" I asked.

"I lost my son before I could leave him anything. True's got four. It seems fair to help out."

"Help out?" I asked. He was right about being dense. It felt like I was pulling my thoughts out of concrete.

"I'm probably the world's worst and slowest typist but I think it will hold up in court. They had one of those notary stamp things in the director's office. I turned the date stamp thing back to Christmas Day."

"You spent Christmas here too?"

"Yep."

"I didn't know that," I said.

"You didn't ask. Anyways, I'm leaving True's kids some money. Like I said, I didn't spend all of the past three days in the locker room."

"Jerry. That's great. That's just wonderful."

"It's not much. I was going to leave it to the VFW otherwise. True will do something good with it. The VFW, they can have a fundraiser and figure something out."

"Jerry. Thank you."

"Thank you, Alan. See you on the other side some other time. Goodbye."

The fog lifted and Jerry's face faded from view, only to be replaced by a blur of other faces.

Goodbye? That was it? Just goodbye? That couldn't be it. I had so much I needed to say to him still. He was so comfortable with the afterlife even though he didn't seem to believe in it. Maybe that was it. Maybe it didn't matter what happened after death. Maybe it was simply what one did while alive. For however long that was. Jerry didn't seem to mind the unanswered questions. But I had questions. I also had a headache beyond anything I had ever experienced. I fervently hoped he would see Millie and his son again.

The blur of faces were talking nonstop.

"We don't know anyone named Jerry."

"Who was he talking to?"

"How do we know if he stops hallucinating?"

"What if he doesn't recognize us?"

"Who's Jerry?"

"Maybe he means Terry? Does he know a Terry?"

"Wasn't there a Terry in the house across Lake Drive? The couple that moved to Arizona?"

"Jerry," I said again, coughing in another fit, trying to come up with an explanation for them. I was a little offended by the suggestion that I was hallucinating.

"There he goes again," wailed one of the voices.

"Folks, he may need some rest before he can interact with you. I'm going to have you all wait back in the family waiting room. The good news is that Mr. Fries seems to be well on the road to recovery. It's normal for him to be confused for a little while. He's been through a lot. Hopefully he'll be able to talk with all of you a little later."

I saw shadows leave the room. The worried murmurs left with them. I was left alone with the occasional beep from the monitor and drone of the morning news on channel four on the flatscreen perched in the corner of the room.

My eyes wouldn't quite focus but I could make out the silhouette of a woman with news-anchor hair. They played the theme song from the morning news hour.

"The big story this morning is the scandal breaking at St. Augustine's hospital. We go live to Bob downtown for an update."

"Thanks Pam. I'm live outside the county courthouse where a motion for complete disclosure of all financial records was just made by the district attorney. This case really has everybody talking. The DA has called it the worst case of fraud he has seen in his career. It seems the CEO, Belle Evans, as well the chief financial officer for the hospital were both complicit in falsifying records to make St. Augustine's look far more profitable than it really was, all the while cutting staff and taking huge bonuses themselves. But the most distasteful aspect of this concerns a local physician, Dr. Frank Lazarus, who is accused of running a Medicaid mill in which fraudulent procedures were billed on patients who never received them, just to bump up the Medicaid numbers for St. Augustine's."

"Bob, that is truly scandalous. What have we heard in defense from the hospital administration?"

"Well Pam, the board of directors for St. Augustine's really seems to want to get out in front of this. They have promised full cooperation and have supported full prosecution of the individuals involved. We haven't heard anything from Ms. Evans, Dr. Lazarus, or the CFO at this time. Our understanding is that the hospital is under interim leadership while the investigation continues and we expect a statement later today. We will certainly be following this story closely and we will bring you live updates as the day progresses."

I closed my eyes from the glare of the screen and let my mind wander. My hands opened and closed and I ran them lightly over the sheets. We had done it. I coughed again. I had never been so happy to feel like crap before. Jerry's last act of kindness to True's kids, it hadn't been that random, like those bumper stickers said. It all made sense, I thought. I opened my eyes after a few minutes and they focused better. There was another babble of voices in the room. I didn't recognize any of them but I could make out a half dozen people in white coats around the perimeter of the bed. An imperious voice asked "which of you has been following Mr. Fries and would like to present?"

Koala, koala, I thought. Why was I thinking that? Where was Laura? I needed to tell her I wasn't hallucinating.

It came back to me.

I closed my eyes and lay quietly in the bed.

A young man began his presentation. "This is a fifty-two year old male status post ventricular fibrillation arrest who underwent the hypothermia protocol and..."

I coughed loudly and he stopped. I opened my eyes and the perimeter of eyes around the bed stared back.

"It was wasabi peas," I said.

"Beg your pardon, Mr. Fries?"

"It's pronounced fries-as-in-peas. I choked on a wasabi pea. Be careful with those things. I just want to set the record straight."

Behind them the flatscreen was now in clear focus.

"Yes, Bob, this scandal will shake the local hospital community to the core. And who knows what the national implications might be in terms of fraud investigation."

"Pam, we have just learned from the board of directors that we have an anonymous whistleblower to thank for blowing this story wide open. Sources tell us it was a homeless man in the emergency department but we can only speculate that someone was investigating under cover. We'll keep you posted."

The white coated parade shuffled out of my room and I closed my eyes. Thank you, Jerry.

To the readers:

Room Four is a work of fiction. Any resemblance of characters or plot to real people or events is coincidence only. Many thanks to Henry Hungerbeeler, Tom Quedensley, Susanne Hathaway, and Julie Faber who helped edit the much clunkier early versions of this book. Thanks to Mike Munz and Laetitia Patezour, cover model and photographer extraordinaire. Thanks especially to Fiona and Dean, who listen patiently to my stories, tell me even better ones, and make it all worthwhile. I am grateful to my patients and colleagues, who inspire me with their wit, grace, and compassion in very challenging circumstances.

My greatest fear in publishing Room Four is that it comes across as cynical. That was not my intent. The ER is a gritty, hectic place but it is rich in tough love. I hope the kindness of the characters shines through their crass and crusty exteriors. I have tried to capture the background cacophony of the ER, how real people bitch, moan, and cheer each other on. No offense is meant by some of the expressions used. This is not a book for or against religion. I think it can be enjoyed by people of many different beliefs. Over the course of my career I have praised God, cursed God, questioned God and seen my patients do the same. Like Jerry and Alan, I don't have all the answers, but the conversation is always worthwhile. When there isn't time during a shift to contemplate the big questions, I talk it over with my book characters the next day.

With best wishes for health and happiness,
A.J. KNAUSS

ROOM FOUR

www.ajknauss.weebly.com